Deck the Halls with Danger

A Yuletide Novella

Crime Scene Kosovo

Tasmin Turner

Deck The Halls With Danger
A Crime Scene Kosovo Yuletide Novella

by
Tasmin Turner

Also by Tasmin Turner

Available as print on demand ISBN 978-1-7386164-2-8

For more information see www.wish-books.com

Cover Design by 100 Covers

Chapter 1

Shadows in the Snow

*P*ristina, Kosovo

The Christmas market in Pristina was aglow, its colorful lights casting a warm, inviting radiance against the encroaching dusk. Stalls bustled beneath, while a fresh layer of snow added a sparkle to the scene, its glistening patches reflecting the joyous mood. The air was ripe with the mingling scents of spiced mulled wine and resinous pine trees, a sensory shield against winter's bite. Laughter and chatter filled the space as families, friends, and wanderers alike contributed to the market's festive spirit. Vendors, with a twinkle of holiday cheer, showcased their handcrafted wares and seasonal treats, luring onlookers with the allure of their aromatic and visual feast.

Amid the seasonal cheer, international lawyer Kit Chase stood, her auburn hair hidden beneath a snug beanie, her hands wrapped around a cup of steaming mulled wine.

Her turquoise eyes flickered across the crowd, a part of her yearning to surrender to the festive spirit enveloping her. At her side, Owen Reese exuded a reassuring presence. Dressed in a fitted jacket that complemented his sturdy build, he kept a close eye on her every move with his piercing dark-blue gaze, never missing a beat. She felt safe and protected by his strong presence.

For a moment, Kit allowed the festivity to eclipse her ever-present tension that tethered her to the rigorous demands of her job as an international prosecutor in Kosovo —a role that often put her at personal and professional risk in pursuit of justice. This evening, the holiday ambiance almost made her forget those looming responsibilities. Owen caught her gaze, his look conveying a silent pact: to set aside the world's burdens and bask in the present moment. In that fleeting connection, Kit discovered a fragile sanctuary of tranquillity amid the market's ambiance.

Taking a cautious sip of the mulled wine, she welcomed the liquid warmth as it seared her lips, then soothed her from within, quieting the relentless thoughts that shadowed her life as an international prosecutor.

"So, Owen," Kit ventured, a playful tone in her voice as she shifted toward him. "How do you celebrate Christmas back in Cardiff?"

The corners of Owen's eyes crinkled with the joy of fond memories. "Oh, it's all about family traditions," he said with a soft Welsh cadence. "My grandmother takes charge of the kitchen—roast turkey, stuffing, and her famous fruit mince pies. We all converge at her house in the morning and make a day of it, feasting, unwrapping gifts, and the inevitable squabbles over board games."

Kit imagined the scene—so different from her summer-time Christmases in New Zealand, yet equally heartwarming. "That sounds wonderful, Owen. We tend to spend it outdoors, you know, with the sun shining overhead. Barbecue on the beach, seafood on the grill, and some beach cricket for good measure. This year, my cousin Paige is visiting me here in Pristina."

Owen's smile grew warmer, as if the thought of Christmas on a beach delighted him. "That's quite the contrast to a Welsh winter. Sounds brilliant, though."

Standing beside the mulled wine stall, the miles between Cardiff and Auckland seemed to dissolve. Here they were, a prosecutor from New Zealand and a military police sergeant from Wales, finding common ground amid the unique camaraderie the season offered. They toasted with their mugs, the rich scent of spices momentarily lifting the burden of their duties.

In that next sip of mulled wine, Kit felt a wave of tranquility, a fleeting escape from the high stakes of international justice. She was momentarily home, not in a place, but in spirit. And as she locked eyes with Owen, they shared an unspoken bond—a silent pact of solidarity in their shared uncertainty.

Nostalgia softened Kit's expression. "Years ago, my dad, Vernon, was the grill master, while Mum would whip up her pavlova masterpiece. After Vernon moved to Australia, things ... shifted."

Owen offered a sympathetic nod. "You mentioned Vernon's come back into your life."

"Yeah, he played a key part in extraditing Simić for war crimes. He even managed to stick around for Halloween, and helped us with some critical intel on Black Sun," she said, her past colliding with the present.

As they spoke, the intricate pattern of Kit's life seemed to unfold before them, each part woven with victories and sorrows. Owen's intent gaze held hers, an unspoken promise of understanding and refuge within it. His voice dropped to a whisper. "I feel like kissing you, Kit." A pause lingered between them, charged with unspoken emotion. "But, perhaps that's a moment best saved for later."

A wave of exhilaration washed over Kit, Owen's words anchoring her in a serenity seldom found amidst their turbulent lives.

"I'd welcome that," she answered, her gaze locking with his in a silent agreement. "I just need to pick up a few festive ornaments, then we can head back," she suggested, savoring the final warming sip of her wine. "We've got a Secret Santa at the office. Any ideas on what to get?"

"Something meaningful yet appropriate. It's a delicate balance," he advised with a thoughtful tilt of his head.

"Exactly," she echoed, a contemplative smile touching her lips. "What about your plans for Christmas?"

His smile held a deeper intimacy, revealing the value he placed on their shared time. "Being here in Pristina, with you—it's where I want to be."

They began their leisurely walk back to her apartment, nestled within a stone's throw from the lively town center. Kit experienced an unfamiliar contentment; for the first time in ages, Christmas felt like an imminent delight rather than a distant memory.

The festive bustle of Pristina's Christmas market was a celebration of unity, bridging cultural divides in a predominantly Muslim city of diverse faiths. Laughter and warm exchanges knit the cold air as people from all walks of life reveled in the holiday spirit.

Kit navigated the snowy walkways with confidence, her puffer jacket enveloping her and protecting her against the bracing cold, its hue a subtle complement to her fiery hair.

Her steps, purposeful and steady, marked a rhythmic counterpoint to the soft crunch of snow beneath her boots.

Owen dressed in a blend of police officer and civilian. His jeans bore the marks of an active life, while his knitted Welsh sweater told stories of home and heritage. He wore his EUFOR jacket over his personal clothing, its emblem a constant reminder of his professional identity.

As they weaved through the bustling market stalls, Kit's gaze was abruptly intercepted by an advancing figure. Major Matthew Hackman, his presence a stark contrast to the merry scene, approached them with a determined stride. The sense of urgency emanating from him cast a shadow over the festive lights, signaling trouble. Kit's stomach tightened; impromptu visits from Matt, especially as Owen's superior and with his ties her boss, Eva Refazo, were rarely harbingers of good news.

Dressed in practical military fatigues designed for resilience against both weather and wear, Matt advanced through the market. His heavy boots imprinted deep marks in the snow, and his weathered jacket offered little concession to the biting cold. His demeanor, serious and unyielding, disrupted the surrounding holiday cheer.

"Evening, Kit, Owen," he greeted, his tone grave, confirming Kit's suspicions. "Sorry to cut into your downtime, but we have an urgent situation."

Owen's posture shifted to full alert. "What's going on, Major?"

Matt scanned their surroundings for prying ears before continuing, "I need you both to come with me immediately. Eva's been in touch; your office's assistance is required."

Kit's heart sank. "This sounds dire," she murmured, seeking any hint in his expression, but finding none. A chill of foreboding crept into her, overshadowing the holiday joy.

Matt's somber tone was all too familiar—one that could unravel the festive season and possibly spell tragedy.

With Matt leading, they moved away from the lively market to a secluded area cordoned off by police tape. Acknowledging nods were exchanged with the officers, who lifted the cordon for them to pass.

The scene that confronted them was chilling—a man, no older than his mid-thirties, lay motionless under a partial blanket of snow. Strands of dark-medium brown hair peeked from beneath a woolen cap, and his waterlogged leather boots spoke of his ill-fated journey through the snow. Kit's eyes were drawn to his lifeless gaze, an ugly wound marring his face, telling a silent story of his final struggle. The discolored bruising and the foam at his mouth were ominous indicators of his last moments—unlikely to be from natural causes.

The familiar terra firma of certainty seemed to shudder under Kit's feet, forcing her to latch onto the harsh truth that lay bare before them. Her prosecutor's instincts surged as Owen steeled himself for the grim task at hand. The merry ambiance that had cloaked the city was now marred by the sinister presence of a serious crime.

Kit's fingers were steady as she dialed Eva, her voice a measured blend of alarm and control. "Eva, it's Kit. There's a body—an unidentified man—down by the Christmas market. Indications of foul play, possibly poison. No ID. It's messy."

Eva Refazo's response, laced with a hint of her Italian heritage, sliced through the static with a crisp directive. "Understood. I was already informed. Please make sure the perimeter is secure. CSU is on its way to process the scene.

Confirm death, but leave the rest to the coroner. Dr. Prabhu will take it from there. Please keep me informed."

With the call ended, the reality of their task settled heavily upon them. The holiday season had transformed into an all-too-familiar scene of investigation. Kit snapped her phone shut, a sense of resignation replacing what had been an anticipated evening. "Well, there goes our night," she said with a wry smile, catching Owen's eye as he received a quiet briefing from Matt.

The Crime Scene Processing Unit had arrived promptly, donning their sterile white suits like a team of forensic surgeons. They worked around the body meticulously, collecting potential evidence—hair samples, fibers, and scraping for any trace DNA under the victim's nails. Kit and Owen stood by, observing the careful preservation of the scene.

Owen, his eyes flickering between Kit and the crime scene, voiced a regret that mirrored her own. "Was hoping for a more peaceful evening," he said. "Now Matt's got me swamped with reports."

Kit nodded towards the body, her own responsibilities casting a shadow over the festive spirit. "Eva's got me on the follow-up with the coroner's office," she replied.

Owen gave her hand a reassuring squeeze, brief yet meaningful. "Catch up later, yeah? Hopefully under better circumstances," he said before heading off to join Matt, who was already on a call, his expression grave.

Left alone, Kit's attention was drawn back to the scene. A nagging intuition whispered for her to take another look. As Owen's car pulled away, she approached the cordoned area once more. Her flashlight beam danced across the snowy ground and halted on a faint glint partially buried in the white. Crouching down, she carefully unearthed a battered flash drive with a serpentine design encircling a mysterious emblem—a symbol she recognized all too well.

A memory flashed: a recent case involving the Black Sun—a pan-European network with visions of reviving a bygone empire and undermining peace. The potential link between this extremist group and the current murder, especially at this time of year, sent a shiver through her. Kit pocketed the flash drive, the gravity of its implications settling in. The idea that these radicals could be active again, especially so close to Christmas, was a chilling prospect she hoped fervently was not the case.

Crossing the threshold of her apartment, Kit was enveloped by its tranquil Scandinavian aesthetic—a welcome respite from the day's grim discoveries. The living room was a testament to her minimalist tastes, with a curated selection of classic detective novels and legal tomes resting on the shelf, their worn spines a portal to worlds of intrigue and justice. The kitchenette, modest but efficient, boasted a kettle and coffee maker alongside a bowl of fresh fruit—a vibrant splash of color against the muted tones of the room. Here, within these walls, the chaos of the outside world receded, replaced by the comfort of familiar surroundings.

Shedding her coat, Kit moved purposefully towards the kitchenette. She hesitated briefly, caught between the lure of herbal tea's promise of tranquility and the stark wakefulness offered by a robust coffee. Decision made, she watched the dark Americano coffee cascade into her cup, the rich aroma a silent vow of sustained alertness through the night's impending tasks. With each swirl of the brew, the etched markings on the flash drive beckoned, an enigmatic echo of the Black Sun's emblem that she couldn't dismiss.

Mug in hand, Kit sank into the embrace of her couch, allowing herself a moment to breathe before powering up the secure laptop designed for such critical moments—air-gapped, unassailable by digital threats. She initiated the advanced decryption software, a tool from her prosecutorial arsenal, and waited. The drive might contain mundane data or, as she feared, the key to unlocking the shadows over Pristina.

The screen blinked to black, a momentary void that stretched into an eternity of anticipation. Then, it flickered to life, revealing a directory ominously titled "Siberian Vipers_Ops." Kit's heartbeat quickened as she double-clicked, and before her eyes unfurled a labyrinth of clandestine information.

To balance the intensity of her dive into the encrypted secrets, she retrieved a container of yogurt from the fridge, the simple act grounding her amid the surge of adrenaline. Placing it beside her laptop, she donned her reading glasses —a new necessity that marked the passage of time more than she cared to admit. With a focused gaze through the lenses, Kit prepared to unravel the encrypted enigmas now laid bare before her.

Kit's focus narrowed on a document highlighting a log of covert informants—a cache of intelligence on the Siberian Vipers' clandestine operations. One entry, marked in fluo-rescent virtual ink, indicated a meeting with an individual identified only as S. Sokolov. The rendezvous was sched-uled at Kafja e Përfshtuar—"The Perfect Coffee"—an incon-spicuous Pristina café known more for whispered secrets than its espresso blends, set for the morning after next.

She lingered on a complex spreadsheet labeled "Off-shore Accounts_Eclipse." Rows of encrypted numbers cascaded down, interwoven with substantial balances and intricate transaction histories. Initially, nothing seemed amiss until a repeating pattern emerged—a hallmark of sophisticated money laundering. The alias "Eclipse" tantalizingly hinted at connections to the Black Sun's elusive leader. Yet it was the initials "JM" that resonated with an ominous familiarity. However, it was S. Sokolov's name that seized her full attention. Could it be Sergei Sokolov, whose history with her was woven with passion, conflict, and the specter of an Interpol Red Notice suspended by her intervention?

Sergei's presence in Pristina was a disquieting thought. Their shared history was fraught with complexities, including the esoteric philosophy of khash that he had introduced her to—a clandestine doctrine rooted in the strategic teachings of Rasputin, which had helped her navigate perilous situations. Despite being burned by Sergei's manipulations, his enigmatic allure was undeniable. His absence now, knowing he was within reach, left her with a pang of betrayal mingled with anticipation. Sergei was a chess player at heart, and his silence could well be a calculated maneuver—a play for protection they both might need.

With the café meeting imprinted in her mind, Kit delved deeper into the financial labyrinth. She traced the digital fingerprints that spanned across the grid of transactions, stumbling upon a series of cryptic communications linked to an entity code-named "S. Vipers." The moniker was unfamiliar, yet it resonated with the same dark frequency as Black Sun's network.

Kit initiated a clandestine search, her actions concealed by layers of digital anonymity. The screen became a mosaic of articles, criminal dossiers, and hidden threads of conversation, painting a stark picture of the Siberian Vipers—a nefarious syndicate with a portfolio spanning illicit trades, contract killings, and the art of chaos engineering across Eastern Europe.

A chilling realization settled over her as she pieced together the grim picture. If Sergei was indeed enmeshed with both the Black Sun and the Siberian Vipers, the potential breadth of his influence was alarming. The implications of such an alliance sent a wave of dread through her. This was a convergence of shadows that could engulf the entire region in its dark tide.

Kit shut down the laptop, her reflection momentarily captured on the now-dark screen. The complexities of Sergei's potential involvement in the criminal web left her mind swirling with speculation and unease. If S. Sokolov was indeed Sergei, the likelihood of his deep cover operations for Russian intelligence was high. She had learned long ago that Sergei's moves were often shrouded in shadowy motives.

Her fingers tapped rhythmically against the couch's armrest as she grappled with a choice that danced on the knife-edge of protocol. The thumb drive in her hand was more than physical—it meant decisions yet to be made. Protocol demanded the immediate surrender of evidence, but there was more at stake than procedure. The prospect of revealing Sergei, and possibly jeopardizing his cover, wrestled with her conscience.

Her gaze fell upon the robust safe tucked beneath her bookshelf, a bastion of undisclosed truths. Could she justify delaying the thumb drive's introduction into the evidence pool, ostensibly "finding" it later in a way that shielded Sergei? The thought hovered perilously close to the precipice of legality—a familiar territory for her.

The question of confiding in Owen loomed large. Trust

was the bedrock of their relationship, both professionally and personally, but there were aspects of her past with Sergei that she had never revealed, not even to Owen. How much could she divulge without casting a shadow of doubt over her own integrity?

After a moment of fraught consideration, Kit opened the safe and secured the thumb drive within its steel confines. The rapid drumbeat of her pulse echoed the gravity of her decision. Walking this tightrope between her clandestine history with Sergei and her obligations as a prosecutor was treacherous, but it wasn't unfamiliar territory.

Kit recognized the delicate balance she had to maintain—protecting Sergei's operational secrecy for now, while not compromising her duty. The risks were inherent, the path fraught with potential pitfalls, yet she was determined to chart her course with care, preserving her autonomy and safeguarding the many facets of her complex life.

Chapter 2

The Dead Speak

As she pulled into the morgue's parking lot, the stark modernity of its structure stood in stark contrast to the haunting memories that lingered in Kit's mind. She couldn't escape the echoes of her first major case in Kosovo—the haunting images of the victims, the innocence lost. Though she'd grown more resilient with each case, the specter of that initial trauma enveloped her anew each time she approached the morgue.

A moment of hesitation gripped her within the car's confines, the familiar twinge of apprehension constricting her chest. She took a moment, fists clenched then released, breathing in deeply to steady herself before stepping out into the chilly morning air. With each determined step towards the entrance, she felt a measure of victory over the shadows of her past.

As Kit crossed the threshold, Dr. Jyoti Prabhu was there to greet her—a striking figure with her diamond nose stud glinting beneath intelligent, kohl-rimmed eyes. Her hair, impeccably coiled into a chignon, and the dignified fit of her white coat over vibrant attire spoke of a professional who carried the weight of her knowledge gracefully.

"Good morning, Kit," Dr. Prabhu offered warmly, her smile a counter to the sterile institutional setting. "I've completed the autopsy on your John Doe. If you're prepared, we can review the findings now."

Kit nodded, bracing herself as they passed into the autopsy suite. The antiseptic tang of the morgue hit her, the gleam of stainless steel under harsh lights a stark reminder of the reality they faced. Yet it was the solitary examination table, now ominously empty, that drew her gaze.

Beside the table, Dr. Prabhu began without preamble, "We found peculiarities during the external examination." She hesitated. "Plus, the toxicology report has just come in. There's something you need to see."

Kit focused, letting her prosecutor's intuition cut through any remaining apprehension. "Show me," she said firmly, prepared to chase the truth hidden within the grim details.

Dr. Prabhu, with a nod of understanding, pulled back the shroud of the body bag. "Our John Doe was Caucasian, mid to late thirties," she detailed clinically, pointing to the evident bruising and the suggestive abrasions on his wrists. "These suggest he might have been restrained at some point before his death."

Kit's resolve hardened as she observed the man's bruised face, now tranquil in death, his previously open eyes now shuttered and unreadable. The stark reality of the morgue, with its silenced voices and untold stories, was her arena—an arena where Kit was determined to find justice for the silent.

Dr. Prabhu flipped through the pages clipped to her board, her face somber. "The autopsy showed significant hemorrhaging in the stomach and substantial congestion across the vital organs, including signs of distress in the pharynx and gullet, such as an ulcerated region. Notably, there was mingling of blood within the stomach's contents." Her eyes, steady and serious, met Kit's, signaling the gravity of these revelations.

Kit absorbed the details, her mind aligning each with a piece of a dark puzzle. Dr. Prabhu continued, "The deceased had consumed pastry not long before his death. While no explicit traces of poison were detected, the symptoms are consistent with barbiturate ingestion, or a similar agent. It's murder. The signs are there."

Releasing a breath she hadn't realized she'd been holding, Kit's thoughts raced. She jotted down notes rapidly. The victim could have been held captive, poisoned, then discarded. "Why poison, though?" she pondered aloud. "Physical violence is more common."

Dr. Prabhu considered the question. "Poison can be a silent assassin. It's efficient and can confirm the target's demise with certainty."

Kit's gaze swept the room, memories of past crime scenes filtering through her thoughts. "A gunshot or a stab wound—they're clear evidence, but poison can be subtle."

"Indeed," Dr. Prabhu agreed. "If the right toxin is selected, it could mimic natural causes or delay symptom onset. It allows for a calculated execution—lethal and covert."

Kit contemplated this. "It could be an assertion of power, or perhaps a way to hide the perpetrator's tracks."

"Possibly," Dr. Prabhu concurred. "And if the poison mimics a common condition, it could buy the killers time to vanish."

Kit frowned as she ran a hand through her hair.

"They've sidestepped the obvious indicators of an attack. It's all so coldly premeditated. We need to interpret this message, and swiftly. What if the Russians were involved? What kind of poisons could we be looking at?"

Dr. Prabhu nodded, understanding the implication. "Well, Kit, if we're factoring in that angle, there are a few possibilities that are, let's say, in vogue with Russian operatives. One likely candidate could be a substance like ricin. It's notoriously difficult to trace and is favored for its lethality and the fact that it's a natural compound."

"Anything synthetic?" Kit asked, her pen poised over her notebook.

"Possibly something like polonium-210," Dr. Prabhu suggested, her tone clinical. "It's highly toxic, and even a tiny amount is fatal. It's rumoured to be used in Russian poisonings. Then there's thallium—colorless, tasteless, and equally toxic.

Kit's eyes narrowed. "And these would align with the symptoms you've observed?"

"Yes," Dr. Prabhu confirmed. "Especially if the goal was to ensure the poison wasn't immediately detectable, giving the perpetrator time to escape. However, without a full toxicology report, it's speculative. These are just informed guesses based on the symptoms and history."

"Thank you, Doctor," Kit said, her mind already racing through the implications of these insights.

"The full autopsy report will be in your inbox by the end of the day," Dr. Prabhu assured her.

Kit's thoughts were already on the next step. "What's the estimated time of death?"

"Considering his last meal and the state of the body, I'd estimate his death occurred between twelve thirty and thirteen forty. The body showed signs of a scuffle prior to death, likely close to where he was found," Dr. Prabhu deduced.

"And your reasoning for his death occurring near the discovery site?"

"The absence of postmortem movement and the condition of his attire suggest minimal interference post-death. His clothing was consistent with the immediate environment—no excess soil, foliage, or foreign debris." Dr. Prabhu's analysis was dispassionate yet incisive.

Kit nodded, her mind sifting through the strands of the case. "He was left in that alley off Mother Teresa Boulevard —a perfect balance of exposure and concealment. We'll need to canvas the area thoroughly."

Dr. Prabhu's expression acknowledged the plan. "Yes, if he was left there in broad daylight. Someone might have seen something."

Kit's thoughts flitted to the hidden thumb drive. She could disclose it, sanitize its contents of any ties to Sergei, and offer it up as evidence—a move fraught with risk. Or she could hold onto it, using the information privately to track Sergei's actions. For now, she resolved to keep her knowledge of the drive to herself, sharing with Owen only what was necessary. The deeper web of Sergei's involvement, for the moment, remained hers alone to untangle. For now, that thumb drive stayed exactly where it was, locked away and out of reach.

Dr. Prabhu's voice cut through Kit's thoughts. "There's something else you should see."

Kit refocused on her. "What have you found?"

"Look here," Dr. Prabhu said, pulling back the sleeve of the corpse's left arm and shining a UV light over the skin. Under the light, a sequence of Cyrillic letters fluoresced an unnatural blue, marking the flesh with an intention that belied its secretive placement.

Kit's breath hitched. "Can you read it?"

"It's not my area of expertise. Russian, perhaps?" Dr. Prabhu guessed, her eyebrows knitting in a mixture of curiosity and concern.

Kit quickly snapped a photo with her phone. "I'll find someone who can translate this. But how did you come upon it?"

"During the external exam, I noticed a discoloration. It wasn't consistent with the other bruising. UV light sometimes reveals what's invisible to the naked eye," Dr. Prabhu explained, her professionalism underscoring the importance of her find.

Kit's eyes then caught another detail, a symbol nestled near the cryptic text—a wheel with radiating rays. "The Black Sun," she murmured, recognition dawning on her.

Dr. Prabhu angled the light to better reveal the design. "Is it significant?"

"Very," Kit replied. "It's tied to a case I worked on recently involving a neofascist network. This could be a key piece of evidence."

The gravity of the situation settled in as Dr. Prabhu met Kit's gaze. "If he inscribed this on himself, it was meant to be found. It's deliberate."

Kit nodded solemnly, the meaning of the discovery settling in. "Exactly. And this Black Sun symbol alongside it —it's a dire portent."

A chill seemed to sweep through the morgue as they stared at the luminescent writing, the UV light casting an otherworldly glow on the cryptic message.

"This implies that his death could be linked to larger, more sinister machinations. Given this group's history, we may not have much time," Kit said, urgency lacing her voice. "I need to get this translated right away."

Dr. Prabhu looked on, her expression somber. "Let me know if you need any further assistance."

As Kit pocketed her phone, her resolve solidified. She knew just who to contact for the translation—a step closer to unraveling the mystery that now lay before them, shrouded in shadow and secrecy.

Chapter 3

Frequencies of Forensics and Faith

Kit gripped the steering wheel tighter as her OIDC vehicle snaked through the serpentine roads to Visoki Dečani Monastery. The solitude of the journey was her choice, but it came at a cost. Natalia had been her companion on past visits to this place of refuge, her presence a comfort that Kit now found herself missing. And Owen ... Owen had a way of simplifying the complex, which in cases like these, where every shadow mattered, could be less than helpful.

There were corners of her life, like her past entanglement with Sergei Sokolov, that remained shrouded, much like the valleys and peaks that cradled the monastery away from the prying eyes of Pristina. Today's visit was a solitary venture to meet Father Peter, the man who bridged the gap between the Russian Orthodox and the Serbian Orthodox churches, specializing in artifact preservation.

Kit had prepared for the visit with care, choosing attire that melded respect with functionality: a long skirt, a tunic, and a shawl to cover her head in deference to Orthodox tradition, as was the custom for women visiting the church.

The call confirming her appointment with Father Peter had come promptly, setting the tone for a morning of revelations.

Glancing at the empty stretch in the rear-view mirror, Kit felt a twinge of vulnerability at the lack of a backup—another set of eyes, someone to share the burden of what might unfold. But the risk of Sergei's name emerging in unwanted circles was too great. This was a path she had to walk alone.

When the monastery's ancient silhouette finally crested the horizon, a mixture of apprehension and resolve churned within her. She reflected on the details of John Doe's final hours as shared in Dr. Prabhu's briefing: the contusions and wrist abrasions, and the conspicuous lack of defensive wounds, suggesting a familiarity with his attackers. These intricacies she had relayed to Eva, Major Hackman, and Owen, each absorbing the gravity of the case—except for the contents of the thumb drive, which remained her secret. The Black Sun symbol, found inked near the cryptic message on the victim's arm, was a chilling piece of the puzzle, hinting at radical motivations behind the murder.

As the monastery loomed closer, Kit's determination hardened. Today's meeting might reveal more than just religious artifacts. It might shine light on a shadow that had fallen over her life. "The Black Sun symbol. We saw it before in the Halloween attack case," Kit had reminded her team, watching as Eva's eyes narrowed and Owen's jaw clenched. "Even though our chief suspects in the Halloween terror plot refused to admit a wider conspiracy, intel showed that this goes beyond a single local extremist group."

The thumb drive hidden away in her apartment's safe was a silent testament to Kit's solitary burden—a secret harbinger of truth or disaster. She alone had uncovered it, and that sense of ownership tugged at her, even as her conscience whispered insistently about duty. She would likely surrender it to the authorities, but on her terms, and not before she extracted what she needed from its contents.

As the miles disappeared behind her en route to Visoki Dečani Monastery, Kit mulled over the cryptic message they'd discovered on the body. Father Peter had the knowledge to decipher the Cyrillic script, of that she was certain. But the real question was whether he could unravel the web that tied the ominous Black Sun to the unfortunate individual in Dr. Prabhu's morgue—and do it swiftly.

Her train of thought was abruptly derailed by the ping of her phone. Safety first. She pulled over, keen on any new leads that could bolster her meeting with Father Peter. Information was power, especially now.

Owen's familiar tone filled the vehicle's cabin, his Welsh accent delivering unexpected news through their secure channel. "Anatoly Morozov, a Ukrainian national working for the CIA on covert operations within Balkan organized crime. That's our John Doe," he revealed. "The embassy is tight-lipped, but we're digging deeper."

Stunned, Kit let her phone rest in her lap for a breath, her eyes tracing the undulating landscape of Kosovo. Morozov's identity could explain the cryptic markings. If he suspected his cover compromised, leaving a trail for allies postmortem was plausible.

Before she could fully process the implications, another alert drew her attention back to the screen. A message from Dr. Prabhu flashed: "More inscriptions on our John Doe. Names 'Mueller' and 'Sokolov' found, alongside a Black Sun symbol."

Her pulse quickened. "JM"—those initials from the

thumb drive, now ominously linked to Jacob Mueller, the disgraced former head of OIDC she'd helped to arrest. And "Sokolov"—the name that always caused her heart to skip, tied to a past she couldn't fully leave behind. These revelations demanded her full attention, but first, she had an appointment to keep.

Kit pulled up to the formidable gates of Visoki Dečani Monastery, a bastion of serenity amid a land rife with contention. Surrounded by the watchful presence of EUFOR soldiers, the monastery's historical resonance offered a stark contrast to the complexities swirling in Kit's thoughts.

She guided her vehicle towards the monastery's checkpoint, where the vigilant gaze of EUFOR personnel, their arms evident but not imposing, met her arrival. After parking, Kit observed a group of tourists spilling from a bus, cameras eagerly in hand. The monastery stood as a paradox in stone—a sanctuary veiled in stillness, surrounded by the murmuring of a living history.

Exiting her car, the weight of centuries seemed to press upon Kit, the political echoes of Kosovo and Serbia's disputes mingling with her own clandestine burdens. She steeled herself as she walked toward the monastery's entry, the place where Father Peter—keeper of both artifacts and secrets—awaited.

Identification in hand, Kit was granted passage without delay. Her footsteps resonated against ancient cobblestone, the metal door graced with Orthodox crosses creaking open to admit her. Once inside, the monastery unfolded its historical grandeur: a stone church that stood as much a bastion as a sanctuary, its narrow windows and robust doors a testament to both faith and fortitude.

Passing into the monastery's hallowed halls was akin to

traversing centuries. Memories of her last visit with Natalia, confronting relic thieves, flickered in her mind. It was here that Father Peter had first introduced her to the enigmatic ways of khash philosophy, binding her closer to the mysterious Tracer Fox—a guide through the game of shadows and strategy.

A figure approached, his black robes flowing along the stone floors, his presence as commanding as the icons that adorned the walls. Father Peter, with his distinctive clerical hat and a beard flecked with wisdom's silver, greeted her. Kit's pulse quickened, recognizing the priest who was as much a sage as a restorer and custodian of relics.

"Ms. Chase, welcome." Father Peter's voice resonated with a timbre that seemed to echo off the stone. "This way, please." He led her to a secluded study, a room redolent with the scent of ancient tomes and the subtle fragrance of incense. A chessboard lay in wait, the pieces arrayed in silent anticipation, mirroring the strategic dance Kit knew they were about to engage in.

Kit settled into the chair across from Father Peter, her voice composed despite the urgency of her visit. "I appreciate your willingness to meet today, Father."

Father Peter's gaze fixed on her, sharp and assessing. "What matter requires such haste?"

Kit inhaled slowly, her resolve firm. "We found a murder victim, Father. On his skin was a message written in Cyrillic script, visible only under ultraviolet light. We're at a loss. Could you help decipher it?"

Nodding, Father Peter accepted the phone Kit extended towards him. He studied the image intently, his expression shifting. "This script is Old Church Slavonic, used since the ninth century for sacred texts within the Orthodox tradition."

Kit leaned forward. "Similar to how Latin was used in the Roman Catholic Church?"

"Exactly," Father Peter affirmed. "It has carried the words of the divine across centuries, though its use among the laity has waned."

Kit's curiosity piqued. "And the message?"

Handing back the phone, the gravity in Father Peter's voice was palpable. "It reads, 'The serpents awake.'"

A heavy silence enveloped them, charged with the implications of the phrase.

"'The serpents awake,'" Kit echoed, her mind racing. "Could it be symbolic, perhaps a warning?"

The priest's blue eyes held a glint of concern. "In scripture, serpents often represent malevolence or guile. This could signal the resurgence of hidden threats or the revival of old feuds."

Kit's thoughts darted to her investigation. "Does the name 'Siberian Vipers' mean anything to you?"

Recognition registered on Father Peter's face. "Indeed. They're a notorious faction, their deeds marking them as much more than regular criminals. This use of archaic Slavonic suggests a deliberate obfuscation, a message not meant for casual eyes."

Father Peter leaned back, his expression serious. "While I serve the Church, I also strive to remain aware of secular threats. The Siberian Vipers are known for their ruthless operations, from trafficking to arms dealing. They're like a hydra—cut off one head, and two more grow in its place. Be wary, for their reach may extend further than you suspect, and their motives are surely complex."

Kit nodded. "Thank you, Father. That's helpful."

"Go carefully," he advised. "You tread a path lined with shadows, and the light of truth may well cast darker ones.

Kit leaned forward, her eyes intent. "The choice of Old Slavonic—do you think the victim was trying to ensure his message would reach the right eyes after his death?"

Father Peter pondered for a moment. "It's likely he anticipated the involvement of someone familiar with the script, perhaps even someone from within these very walls." He gestured to the ancient tomes that surrounded them.

"Could it be a message meant only for the eyes of someone within his cultural or religious circle?" Kit asked, her mind racing with possibilities.

"Quite possibly," Father Peter conceded. "It adds a layer of encryption by using a language only a select few could decode today."

"Or could it be a deliberate red herring, intended to mislead investigators?"

"That's also plausible," he replied. "In matters such as these, every detail can be a cipher or a decoy."

"And the message itself—it was directed at someone specific?" Kit probed further.

"It's possible," Father Peter mused. "The use of such a historically and spiritually significant language suggests a direct, if not intimate, communication. It's meant for someone who understands its legacy."

Kit's gaze held a new intensity. "And the emotional implications of the message?"

"The language's sacred roots could elevate the message's perceived sanctity, imbuing the victim's final words with a gravitas only a few could truly comprehend."

"So, we're looking at a significant choice," Kit said.

"Indeed," Father Peter agreed. "Such a choice is never incidental."

Kit shifted the conversation. "On a related note, the

coroner found Morse code on the body. It mentioned 'S. Sokolov.' Could that be Sergei?"

The priest's composure briefly flickered. "Sergei, you say? His path has always been ... labyrinthine. But to my knowledge, he operates with a certain honor."

"Any possible link between him and this murder?" Kit watched him carefully.

Father Peter shook his head solemnly. "Not that I am aware of. But Sergei's games are intricate, his strategies profound."

Feeling the gravity of Father Peter's words, Kit swiftly changed the subject.

"On another topic," she whispered, leaning closer, "I've been looking further into khash, guided by the Tracer Fox. I feel I need greater insight."

Father Peter's expression warmed. "The Tracer Fox is an exceptional mentor for navigating life's chessboard. It sounds like you're ready for some deeper lessons."

"Yes, I think I am," Kit affirmed.

Reaching into a drawer, Father Peter produced a worn notebook. "Here are meditations I've compiled, integrating scriptural wisdom, chess tactics, and vibrational study to refine one's strategic perception."

Kit accepted the notebook with a nod, planning to explore every page. "Thank you, Father. This could be the key to unlocking more secrets."

The priest smiled. "Indeed, Ms. Chase. Sometimes, the most profound insights are found where we least expect them."

Kit's curiosity was piqued as she pored over the marked page, where ancient verses interlaced with strategic plays and resonant numbers suggested a novel approach to contemplation. "Intriguing," she murmured. "How do these apply in practice?"

Father Peter carefully removed a sheet from the back of the notebook, its edges worn from frequent handling. "Commit these to memory," he advised gently, his voice imbued with wisdom. "They are keys to unlocking a deeper level of understanding."

The words before Kit seemed to bridge the gap between the mystical and the tactical. The priest held her gaze, imbuing his next words with significance. "Consider these frequencies as guides, sharpening your intuition. Combined with the verses here, they will enhance your focus during meditation, amplifying your insights."

Kit nodded, the concept resonating with her. "So, blending these frequencies with the passages augments clarity?"

"Indeed," he affirmed with a sagacious nod. "It's a practice that hones your discernment, equally effective in analytical deduction or the intricate dance of khash.'

Her lips quirked into a half-smile. "And for the upcoming holidays? Anything in particular you'd recommend?"

His smile broadened, eyes twinkling. "While we observe the Nativity later in the year, these practices are timeless. But for a season of reflection, this sequence here"—he pointed to a passage marked with a star—"is especially potent."

Kit thumbed the page, feeling as if she'd been handed a map to a treasure she'd always sought but never fully grasped.

. . .

Title: "Deck the Halls & Double Attack" - Frequency 852 Hz

Meditation: "Every good and every perfect gift is from above" (James 1:17).

Chess Strategy: Double attack, leveraging the art of simultaneously targeting two threats, mirrors the richness of life's simultaneous chances.

Essence: This tactic exemplifies the strategic balance between risk and reward, aligning one's actions with the precision of a seasoned player.

Frequency: 852 Hz, pivotal in restoring equilibrium, dispelling the haze of confusion, and syncing with the universe's majestic symmetry.

"Got it," Kit said. "Anything for my Tracer Fox?"

Father Peter scribbled on the manuscript. "This one's custom-made," he said, satisfied.

"Silent Night & The Underdog Gambit" - Frequency 528 Hz

Meditation: "The battle is the Lord's, and he will give all of you into our hands" (1 Samuel 17:47).

Chess Strategy: The underdog strategy reflects life's unexpected turns, where the seemingly weak can succeed over adversity.

Essence: Tracer Fox embodies the stealth and shrewdness required to overcome a stronger adversary.

Frequency: 528 Hz, resonates with the heart, weaving peace and fostering transformation within.

.   .   .

She traced the lines of the meditation with a fingertip, pausing on the mention of David and Goliath. "So, it's about outwitting rather than overpowering. And the frequency, five hundred twenty-eight hertz, enhances that concept?"

Father Peter nodded. "Precisely. That frequency is said to facilitate repair and harmony within the body and mind, aligning with the theme of overcoming seemingly insurmountable challenges."

Kit smiled, the corners of her eyes crinkling with appreciation. "That's exactly the kind of edge I need," she replied, her voice tinged with a mixture of excitement and respect. "I can't thank you enough."

He held her gaze warmly. "Take these meditations at your own pace, Kit. They are potent, infused with years of wisdom and prayer. Absorb them gradually, and they will offer you more than just insight. They can transform perception."

In the room's hushed ambiance, Kit sensed the layers of history and knowledge contained within the stone walls, now shared with her.

"Consider the frequencies as harmonies that resonate with your intentions during meditation," Father Peter continued. "The numerical sequences represent specific vibrational frequencies. When played, they align with and enhance the essence of the biblical texts and strategies included here."

Father Peter paused, his expression one of gentle encouragement. "Use these frequencies to set the tone for your reflections or investigative preparation. They will tune your mind to the nuances of the situations you face."

A palpable sense of expectation filled Kit. She felt empowered, holding what felt like an ancient key to a modern quest. "I'm ready to dive in. And the hymns you mentioned, can I find recordings?"

"Orthodox services are replete with such hymns, each resonating with these frequencies. Additionally, many sound healers and therapists can provide recordings or sessions tuned to them," Father Peter suggested with a thoughtful nod. "But begin with 'The Cherubic Hymn'; it holds a special place in our services and is imbued with profound resonance."

"I'll reach out to Natalia then," Kit resolved, already considering the potential resources at her disposal.

"Very good," Father Peter replied.

Kit's eyes returned to the notebook, each entry woven with ancient lore and keen insights. The promise of these meditations felt perfectly timed, offering her the depth and precision she sought for the challenges of the season.Then, remembering another crucial piece of the puzzle, she brought up the image on her phone. "There's something else. This symbol was also on the victim. The Black Sun. What can you tell me about it?"

Father Peter's expression sobered as he regarded the symbol on her screen. "The Black Sun emblem has unsettling connotations. In some circles, it symbolizes rebirth or new beginnings, but it has been appropriated by extremist groups. It's troubling to see it here, on the victim. It may indicate that the deceased was involved with or targeted by a group aligned with far right wing ideologies."

Kit took in the information. "I see. That accords with my information, and it's another worrying layer to our case."

"Be cautious, Kit," Father Peter warned. "The symbol's presence could suggest ties to radical factions. Your journey to uncover the truth may take you into the darkness."

The room charged with a palpable tension, as if they'd

both tapped into a hidden frequency. Kit glanced at the list of meditations, then back at Father Peter. For a moment, religious labels evaporated, eclipsed by a mutual hunt for something far more elusive—a truth neither scripture nor strategy could fully define.

"I have another question for you." Father Peter leant in, eyes intense, and said, "It's about trust. How do we know where to place it?"

Kit's eyes met Father Peter's, absorbing the significance of the question. A taut silence stretched between them. "Trust for me is a calculated risk," she finally replied. "In my line of work, misplaced trust could mean the difference between life and death. What do you think, Father?"

"You've answered your own question," Father Peter said, leaning back in his chair and steepling his fingers. "It is a calculated risk. And in your world, trust can be layered with ulterior motives, secret agendas. In my world, trust starts with faith—faith that despite the sin and grime, there's still something divine in all of us."

As they continued to discuss matters of khash philosophy, life's chessboard, and the ominous Black Sun symbol, Kit felt a connection. Father Peter transcended the role of spiritual adviser, touching on chords Kit hadn't realized needed resonance. She wasn't Russian Orthodox, but in that moment, boundaries of doctrine seemed to fade, replaced by an urgent quest for truth that both their souls recognized.

Father Peter's eyes moved as if he was scanning a chessboard that only he could see. "Imagine a web. Each strand is a different faction, be it organized crime, religious cults, or rogue operatives. They're interwoven in a lattice of alliances and rivalries. It's never static; the web trembles with every move."

His hand cut through the air, slicing the invisible threads. "Now, add to this volatile mix the venom of corruption, the seduction of power, and the allure of forbidden knowledge. It becomes a deadly cocktail. Once stirred, it seeps through the web, affecting everyone entangled in it. The poison is near impossible to contain."

Kit felt the metaphor sink in, bringing with it a sobering clarity. This was not just a war fought with bullets and strategy; it was a complex battleground of shifting loyalties and invisible threats.

"Yes, poison, literally as well as figuratively," she said. "What about Sergei? Do you think I can trust him?"

Father Peter's eyes clouded for a moment, his gaze drifting to a distant point as if weighing invisible scales. Finally, he met Kit's gaze. "Sergei is a complicated individual," he began, his voice tinged with a subtle mixture of affection and caution. "He's like a knight on a chessboard—unpredictable, capable of moves you'd never see coming."

"I've noticed," she said wryly.

He folded his hands, drawing a deep breath. "I've mentored Sergei for years, but even I can't claim to know every room in the labyrinth of his soul. Yes, he has connections to organized crime, but he always said it was a means to an end. However," Father Peter continued, "there are moments when I've caught a certain look in his eyes—a sort of shadow—that suggests his game might extend to other, darker boards. If you're asking whether he could be involved in something more sinister, the honest answer is: I don't know. But it's a possibility you should consider."

The room seemed to close in around Kit. Sergei, the enigma. What game was he playing? And as she knew from past experience, she could not afford to underestimate him.

Father Peter locked eyes with Kit, handing her a small,

worn crucifix. "Take this. You're walking through a labyrinth of shadows, Caitlin. Each corner could hold enlightenment or entrapment. Choose your steps wisely."

As Kit exited the monastery's ancient doors, her footsteps crunching on the gravel pathway, her thoughts whirled with Father Peter's wisdom and warnings. He'd been a cartographer of hidden realms, both external and internal. Kit clenched the small crucifix gifted by Father Peter in her hand. It felt heavier than it looked.

The frequencies and meditations were like tactical assets, she reasoned. The cryptic messages like the Black Sun and "the serpents awake"—those were breadcrumbs in a dark forest, clues to understanding the minds of the suspects. Now she knew what those Cyrillic words said, but she still wasn't sure what the phrase meant, what Morozov was trying to communicate to them. It seemed likely that it was about the Siberian Vipers she had seen referenced in the cryptic thumb drive. Sergei's questionable affiliations, the talk of ancient legacies, organized crime, and cults— these added layers of complexity to an already dangerous game.

But what hit hardest was Father Peter's caution about trust. In a world where the rules constantly shifted, where foes wore the faces of friends, her next move could be a matter of survival.

The deeper she delved, the more she realized that every step was a calculated risk. And as she drove away, she couldn't shake his final words: "Choose your steps wisely." She was out of the sanctuary. The labyrinth awaited. And Kit, gripping the steering wheel tight, knew she was ready to enter.

Chapter 4

Ciphered Shadows

The hush of anticipation in the Office of the International Prosecutor's conference room was palpable as Kit entered. Eva, her focus unwavering on a file before her, sat at the head of the table, while Major Matt Hackman, positioned across, appeared to be lost in thought. Owen, to his right, seemed absorbed in his laptop.

Angel, the office assistant known for her adept multi-tasking, navigated the room with a tray of steaming coffee. "Turkish for a kick or Americano for comfort?" she offered, her tone dancing with a light jest.

"Americano, thanks," Kit replied, claiming the seat adjacent to Eva. As Angel placed a cup before her and retreated with a courteous nod towards Dua Rexhepi, the legal intern poised by the door, Kit prepared mentally for the briefing ahead.

Closing her file with a snap, Eva started the meeting. "Kit, your visit to the monastery—what did you find out?"

Kit straightened in her chair. "If you don't mind, let's first consider the coroner's report. Our victim, identified as

Morozov, a CIA operative, succumbed to what appears to be poison just hours before we found him. Dr. Prabhu found messages on his skin—Old Slavonic script and a Black Sun emblem—only visible with UV light. But there's more," she added, ensuring she had everyone's full attention. "On examination of the deceased's legs with the UV light, I also found the names S. Sokolov and J. Mueller written in Morse code."

Eva leaned in, her tone demanding. "Sokolov and Mueller? Are you suggesting a connection to Jacob Mueller?"

"That's possible," Kit acknowledged. "And adding to the complexity, Father Peter has linked the phrase 'The serpents awake,' found in Old Slavonic on the victim, to the Siberian Vipers, a criminal network with extensive reach."

Owen spoke, his voice somber. "The Vipers aren't just small-time criminals."

Kit glanced around the table. "We're not simply solving a homicide here. This could lead us through a labyrinth of global crime with serious implications."

Matt Hackman's frustration was evident. "The Black Sun again—trouble every time they surface."

"And Sergei Sokolov ... how is he involved?" Owen ventured, the question hanging. "Rumored to be promoted in GRU ranks after his Kosovo operation."

Kit, caught off guard, replied cautiously, "Promoted, you say?"

"We need to pursue that Interpol red notice again, regardless of his diplomatic status," Eva said indignantly.

Kit, steering the conversation from personal history, suggested, "Perhaps revisiting the Black Sun affiliates might yield more information."

Owen agreed, albeit skeptically. "They're tight-lipped

but might volunteer further information with more pressure."

Matt Hackman approved the strategy. "We'll map out the network and relations. A comprehensive murder board is overdue."

Eva shifted focus. "What's the word from Vernon? Any further Five-Eyes intel? He helped us with the last Black Sun case."

Kit deflected. "Nothing current. But speaking of family, my cousin Paige arrives tomorrow for Christmas. I was thinking of introducing her around the office."

Eva gave a nod of assent. "That's fine, as long as it doesn't slow down our cases."

Kit surveyed the conference room, now buzzing with the team's focused debate. She sensed the gravity of their case, a subtle tension between her duty and the need to safeguard her own secrets from the professional world that pressed in from all sides.Kit frowned for a moment and jotted something down on her pad. "It seems like a long time ago when I arranged for Paige's visit. I didn't think the Black Sun and the Siberian Vipers would be rearing their ugly heads so soon."

"I'll look after her, if you like," Dua said, speaking for the first time. All eyes turned to the young Albanian intern who had been sitting quietly taking notes at the end of the table. She had glossy black hair in a bob and warm brown eyes against porcelain skin. She flashed a smile at Kit. "I'd be pleased to let her shadow me. What is she interested in?"

"She's talking about following in the footsteps of her cousin and going to law school. I'm doing my best to talk her out of it," Kit said.

"Why is that?" Dua asked, wide-eyed.

"Nah, not really. It's just my Kiwi sense of humor," Kit

admitted with a grin. "But it's true that if I'd known what it was going to be like practicing law, I might have stuck with sailing around New Zealand. But seriously, Dua, I would be really grateful if you could take Paige under your wing. I've been seriously distracted and haven't planned enough for her visit."

Kit sighed with relief. With all that was on her mind about the latest criminal cases, and Sergei back in town, now a full colonel in the GRU, she had scarcely given Paige a second thought.

"That will be cool . . . like a real family Christmas," Owen said. "Maybe I should invite someone from my family here too."

"No, you don't, Sergeant," Matt said. "I need you to focus on this case. These organized criminal group tentacles must go far beyond isolated events in Kosovo."

"Yes, sir," Owen said automatically, but he waggled his eyebrows at Kit, showing that he hadn't given up on the idea. Kit grinned back at him.

Eva cleared her throat to signal it was time to refocus on the case. "The coroner's report should be coming in today with more details. Let's chase these leads with everything we've got, but watch your backs."

"I've got a team of officers checking buildings around the crime scene and following possible leading regarding the poisoning," Matt said. "I'll let you know if they come up with anything solid."

"That was good work following up with your contact at Dečani Monastery, Kit. None of us is good with ancient Slavonic script," Eva said. "Let's meet again in a couple of days to review progress."

They were about to pack up when Angel cleared her throat. "Sorry to interrupt with such a frivolous matter," she said in her Yorkshire accent. An English rose, Angel was clad in her signature designer jeans and leather jacket over a cashmere sweater. "But just a reminder about the Secret Santa. Don't forget your wrapped gifts for the exchange on Christmas eve. I'll put Paige on the list too, Kit."

Kit acknowledged her with a nod, a flicker of unease passing through her as she considered Paige's upcoming involvement, blissfully unaware of the shadows that were slowly encroaching on them.

Chapter 5

Dark Alliances

D avor Nikolovski conducted a final sweep of security protocols in the Iron Hub, a secluded fortress nestled in the rugged terrain of the Accursed Mountains. As he prepared for a critical video conference, the presence of armed sentinels at the compound's entrance underscored the gravity of the meeting. Behind him, a concise digital network display hummed quietly, pinpointing routes and key locations that mapped out the syndicate's shadowy operations across borders.

Nikolovski's dark, coal-like eyes zeroed in on the two faces that materialized on the screen: Igor Kuznetov of the Siberian Vipers and the pixelated face of a shadowy figure representing the Black Sun, known only as "Operator E."

"Gentlemen, shall we begin?" Nikolovski's voice cut through the static, deep and resonant. "This holiday season, the world will receive a gift that will be long remembered."

His hand poised above the control panel, Davor Nikolovski prepared to unveil the intricacies of their latest scheme. His fingers tapped the touchscreen with the precision of a seasoned tactician. "What you're about to see is the future of our operations in the Balkans," he announced with a measured confidence.

Kuznetov's expression took on an eager anticipation, whereas Operator E maintained a stoic demeanor. Nikolovski's smile, though slight, had the sharpness of a wolf sizing up its prey. They stood on the precipice of a dangerous new era in Kosovo, with Nikolovski orchestrating every move.

"Davor." Igor nodded, industrial machinery in a warehouse visible behind him. "Feels like our days in Chechnya were just yesterday, doesn't it?"

From an undisclosed location in Germany, Operator E's digitized voice cut in. "Time and money are finite. Let's get down to business. I assume the encryption protocols we discussed are in place?"

Davor leaned slightly closer to the camera, his eyes narrowing. "Rest assured, Operator, our conversation is as encrypted as it gets. Only the three of us can hear what's being said. Your concern for confidentiality is well-placed and well-addressed."

Operator E grunted in response. "I trust you have that in hand."

Davor looked directly into the camera. "Back to business. Kosovo is the ultimate crossroads. Imagine, if you will, East meets West right in our backyard, all wrapped up in unreliable borders and pockets of corruption. We're not just operating a hub; we're commanding a gateway."

"Giving access to many doors," Igor Kuznetov smirked. "I miss your theatrics, Davor."

Davor continued, unfazed. "And let's not forget the ongoing tension between Serbia and Kosovo. Their fight is the smoke and mirrors we need. We move in the shadows of nationalist agendas. Trust me, the Serbians would love nothing more than to make Kosovo bleed a little. We give them that, and they give us cover."

Operator E's digitized voice spoke again. "You've always known how to spin geopolitics to advantage, Nikolovski. That's your strength. And one that aligns well with the Black Sun's agenda of far-right supremacy."

Davor leaned in, the intensity of his dark eyes magnified. "Our politics may differ, but we're all in this for the profits. Each of us brings a particular strength to this operation. Black Sun's high-level contacts will ensure smooth logistics and security; Siberian Vipers will handle the intricate network of moving goods. We're each contributing according to our capabilities and will draw profits accordingly."

He swiped his hand across the digital screen behind him, illuminating intricate maps and routes. "As for logistics, we're trafficking in a triad of illicit commodities—heroin, firearms, and human lives. Whether it's Albania, Montenegro, or directly through Serbia, every route has been meticulously planned. We're engineering a well-oiled machine."

"I see it as a labyrinth, with us as the minotaur," Igor growled.

Davor nodded. "Ever one for the mythological references. Exactly so. Our scope is wide. Western Europe is hooked on the heroin; the Middle East never says no to more firepower, and as for human trafficking ... let's just say it's a global market."

Operator E added, "Ambitious. But remember, the higher you build, the less visible you need to be."

Davor leaned back, his eyes narrowing with a wry smile. "Don't worry, Operator E. High visibility may be good for skyscrapers, but for us, it's all about foundations deep in the shadows. We're building an empire, but it's one that will never see the light of day. Trust me, the higher we go, the deeper we'll dig."

Operator E's voice buzzed through the encrypted line, scepticism palpable even through the digital distortion. "Let's not underestimate law enforcement in Kosovo. EUFOR and the international prosecutor's office have been more than a nuisance before. What's your plan there?"

Davor's dark eyes flashed, as if the mere question challenged his mastery of the game. "EUFOR and the prosecutors are manageable. I've got insiders in place. And for those who prove more resistant? They can be dealt with, permanently if need be. Trust me, no one's going to be a thorn in our side."

"And what about the GRU, our 'guardians' here? They have a tendency to meddle." Igor's voice carried a chill as cold as the Siberian air around him.

Davor smiled with assurance. "Ah, Russian Military Intelligence. Rest assured, Igor, we've got several of their operatives on the payroll already. They won't be a problem; in fact, they'll be assets. Your concerns are valid but unnecessary."

Igor nodded, satisfied. "If you've got the GRU in your pocket, then you're ahead of the game, Davor."

Davor leaned into the camera, his eyes smouldering with calculated greed. "We're not talking petty cash here. Within the first year, I estimate our revenue to break the billion-dollar mark. By the third year, we could be looking at five, even seven billion. The profits will be staggering."

Operator E's digital voice commented sceptically, "Those are high numbers, even for this group. And what about the competition? There are other syndicates who'd kill for such a venture."

Davor scoffed. "Let them try. We have geopolitical smokescreens, high-level contacts, and military expertise on our side. Any competing gangs will be inconveniences at best—ones that can be managed."

Igor Kuznetov chuckled. "The Siberian Vipers have faced worse foes and eaten them for breakfast. These gangs don't know who they're dealing with—yet."

Operator E concluded, "The Black Sun's influence runs deep. We'll keep tabs on potential problems through our network within the State apparatus. Make sure the profits roll in, and we'll keep the way clear for our operations."

Davor nodded, the air crackling with the trio's shared ambitions. "Then it's settled. We're in a league of our own, and the world doesn't stand a chance. Let's get to work."

Outlining the crux of their plan, Davor emphasized that the political tensions between Serbia and Kosovo served as a perfect cover for their operations. He planned to exploit this turmoil to move their illicit goods unnoticed, and any shipments that were intercepted by one side could be blamed on the other. As for logistics, he detailed carefully planned routes for trafficking heroin, weapons, and human cargo, offering multiple pathways through Albania, Montenegro, and Serbia. Finally, he spoke about their expansive market reach—from Western Europe to the Middle East and even North America, targeting varying demands for their illegal products.

Leaning back, he locked eyes with the faces on each screen. "My friends, we're not merely constructing an operation. We're forging an empire. An empire whose reach will extend across continents, operating in the shadows and thriving on chaos."

Operator E's digitized voice broke the silence. "Alright, Nikolovski, you present a compelling case. As a Christmas gift to you, we proceed—but don't mistake this for trust. Discretion is everything. Black Sun will be watching."

Igor Kuznetov followed, "I echo that sentiment. The Siberian Vipers don't usually hand out presents, but you've got our conditional support. Keep in mind, the moment this operation threatens to expose us, we're out. Efficiency and stealth, those are the rules."

As the men nodded their conditional agreements on the digital screens, Davor's phone buzzed on the table beside him. He glanced at the incoming message, and his face paled for the first time during the meeting.

"There's something I have to attend to urgently," he muttered, his eyes losing their festive gleam.

Without another word, he reached for his phone, ended the call, and the screens went black.

Chapter 6

Frequencies and Interruptions

K it pulled her apartment door shut behind her, turning the lock with a satisfying click. She draped her jacket on the back of a chair—its form modern yet inviting, like most of the furniture in her minimalist living room.

Tonight was about more than just unwinding. It was about reconnecting with a part of herself that her demanding job couldn't reach. Guided by Father Peter's advice, she was eager to explore the meditations and sound frequencies he'd recommended. She set the kettle to boil, deciding on a cup of chamomile tea for its calming properties. As steam began to rise, she placed a notepad and pen on her low coffee table. The tactile experience of writing had always helped her process thoughts more clearly, and she anticipated needing that clarity tonight.

Finally, she poured the steaming tea into her favorite ceramic mug, its warmth comforting in her hands. She set it down next to the notepad, a prelude to the spiritual journey she was about to undertake. Taking a deep breath, she eased onto her well-worn, yet supportive, couch. For a moment, she closed her eyes, allowing the scent of chamomile to fill her senses, grounding her in the here and now.

Kit reclined on her couch, scrolling to Natalia Marin's contact. Natalia wasn't just a friend; she was an ally in Kit's tangled web of escapades in and around Pristina. A dream therapist with a penchant for the mystical, Natalia's tarot readings and spiritual counsel had become invaluable. Together, they had navigated the treacherous waters of a criminal heist at Dečani Monastery, successfully preserving sacred relics from the clutches of a voracious crime ring. More recently, it was Natalia's penetrating tarot insights that had given Kit the edge in deciphering the shadowy moves behind the Black Sun's terror attack the previous Halloween. Those same insights had been crucial in unraveling the conspiracy and preventing a catastrophe. Kit tapped Natalia's number, her thumb hovering a moment before the final press. There was a certain anticipation, a quiet plea for clarity in the midst of chaos. The phone emitted a rhythmic tone, a countdown to potential revelations.

Her thoughts drifted momentarily to Natalia's place in Dragodan—a convergence of history and innovation, much like Natalia herself, a bridge between the arcane and the actual. The crisp sound of the call connecting cut through Kit's contemplations, pulling her back to the present. She tensed slightly, ready for the voice she trusted to navigate the murky waters they found themselves in time and again.

"Hey, Natalia, it's Kit. You won't believe where I've been—Dečani Monastery. Had to meet Father Peter about a tricky case involving ancient Cyrillic text at a crime scene," Kit spilled, her words tinged with urgency.

"You went to see Father Peter without me?" Natalia's

voice betrayed a flicker of jealousy. "I would've loved to join you."

"I know, I know." Kit sighed. "But the case is complex and dangerous. I had to make a quick trip. On the bright side, Father Peter offered some unique meditations that combine khash philosophy, biblical texts, and specific frequencies."

"Frequencies, you say?" Natalia said, her curiosity piqued.

"Exactly. Take this eight hundred fifty-two hertz one, for instance. Father Peter told me to meditate with it." Kit paused, collecting her thoughts. "Then it hit me. Doesn't someone at the Artemis Healing Center where you work specialize in frequency-based music therapy?"

"You're thinking of Len. He gave me some tracks," Natalia confirmed.

"Any chance you could share them? What if you came over? We could go through Father Peter's notes and try the meditations together," Kit proposed.

"I'm in," Natalia said with enthusiasm. "But you owe me the full monastery story."

"Deal," Kit agreed. "Easier to share in person."

Half an hour later, Natalia stood at Kit's door, a small device in hand. "I've got your eight hundred fifty-two hertz frequencies," she announced, stepping inside. "And just so you know, they're linked to spiritual awakening."

Kit let her in, feeling a twinge of guilt. "I wish I could have invited you to the monastery. It was part of an investigation—sensitive stuff, you know?"

"No worries," Natalia said, setting up the device on the coffee table. "So, what meditation are we going with?"

"Deck the Halls and Double Attack," Kit responded. "The meditation text is from James 1:17, 'Every good gift and every perfect gift is from above.'"

"Ah, so Father Peter tied this frequency to the double attack in chess, where you target two pieces at once. A fitting metaphor for seizing dual opportunities life presents, don't you think?" Natalia smiled, her fingers deftly manipulating a compact amplifier resembling a scaled-down boombox but with a built-in memory card slot. As she activated it, the ethereal sound of the frequency infused the room, a sonic ripple that seemed to hang in the air.

It was as if the universe had aligned its frequencies to bring clarity to Kit's busy mind. The sound was like an auditory tapestry, woven intricately with vibrations that seemed to permeate her body.

Kit glanced at Natalia, who'd stretched out in her chair, eyes closed. Her intuitive friend appeared to be in a state of deep connection, as if conversing with the vibrations themselves. It struck Kit that perhaps Natalia's sensitivity allowed her to comprehend layers of the experience that were veiled to others.

As for Kit, the harmonics slowed her frenetic thought processes, reeling her in from her problem-solving mode. It sharpened her focus onto the words of the biblical verse. With the season of Christmas and the anticipation of Secret Santa looming, the notion of gifts—given and received—took on a newfound significance. Owen came to mind. Kit found herself contemplating the idea of giving him something extraordinary to show him how special he was in her life. After all, her secret stash of discretionary funds was meant for moments exactly like this.

As the 852 Hz frequency continued its work, Kit found her thoughts drifting to the concept of the double attack in chess—a move that simultaneously threatens two pieces, forcing the opponent to choose between losses. It was a concept that Father Peter had intriguingly likened to the multifaceted opportunities that life, and in this case, her investigations, could offer.

On the mental chessboard before her, a bishop chess piece moved in a calculated line, representing the legal trajectory she'd use against the Black Sun and the Siberian Vipers. Her mind's eye then shifted to the knight, that unpredictable piece capable of complex maneuvers, and she couldn't help but see it as a stand-in for Sergei. Was he a piece she could use to her advantage or a rogue element to keep at bay?

And there, in a prominent position, was her queen—the epitome of her own sharp intellect and resilience. This most powerful piece was poised to unravel the convoluted murder case and chase down the killer with her strategic thinking.

But who was the enigmatic black king? Eclipse? Kit sensed his elusive presence on the board, like a shadow looming beyond her immediate sight. His role was undefined, his moves unpredictable, adding an additional layer of complexity to her mental game.

With the room vibrating to the resonance of 852 Hz, Kit felt her mental, emotional, and spiritual levels were aligned, providing her with a newfound clarity. She was ready to tackle her multiple opponents in real life just as she would on the chessboard, with precision and well-considered strategy.

As she began to sink deeper into meditation, her phone buzzed abruptly, snapping her back to reality. She glimpsed the screen, her expression tightening.

"I need to take this," she said, pausing the device and

walking away.

A moment later, she returned, urgency replacing her earlier calm. "We may have a problem," she muttered, looking at Natalia. "Flight delays. Paige won't be here until late afternoon. It's made me aware that I've got to get the place ready for her, as well as juggling things in the office."

Natalia looked at Kit with understanding. "Looks like your meditation was right on cue, huh? A real-life double attack?"

Kit exhaled. "Seems that way. I'd better get ready for tomorrow, but let's meet again soon. How did you find the meditation?"

Natalia leaned back, her eyes narrowing in thought. "Intriguing. I sensed . . .an alignment of sorts. It's given me an idea about incorporating these frequencies into dream therapy—maybe I can use them to enhance intuition in my clients. I could feel their potency, and from the look on your face earlier, I suspect they struck a chord with you too."

Kit raised an eyebrow, intrigued. "They did. You're onto something, Natalia."

Natalia nodded. "Of course. Let's explore this further when you're free. I want to hear more about what Father Peter said."

As they parted ways, with challenges and secrets clouding their paths, the promise of clarity—however fleeting—felt like a gift. As she closed the door behind Natalia, Kit's thoughts accelerated, already shifting gears. Meditation had brought her clarity, but now the complexities of life demanded her attention once more. She had to make her next moves carefully; the stakes were high and the board was set. With her cousin's delayed arrival and a critical stakeout looming, Kit knew it was time to make a double attack.

Chapter 7

A Café of Secrets

The next morning, the engine's hum faded into the frosty air as Kit parked her SUV a block away from *Kafja e Përfshtuar*. Snow crunched beneath her boots, grounding her thoughts. She adjusted the scarf wrapped around her head and slid her sunglasses higher on her nose against the glare of the overcast morning. Trench coat buttoned, she prepared herself for what lay ahead.

Kit's thoughts circled back to Morozov. His final act—leaving behind that secretive thumb drive—had guided her to this stakeout. If he had planned to meet Sergei himself, that confidential rendezvous was now etched in an eerie finality. Today, she'd fill in the void he'd left behind, watching from the shadows for whomever showed up.

As she pushed open the café door, the aroma of coffee mingled with the scents of old wood and worn upholstery. Her eyes scanned the interior—a mix of mismatched furniture and private alcoves shrouded in dim lighting. Glossy, well-worn wooden floors whispered of many private conversations held within these walls.

The barista, a tall man with stubble shadowing his face,

hardly looked up from his espresso machine. He was the epitome of discretion, as if he knew the café's walls held secrets they'd never tell. Kit chose an alcove deep within the cafe, tucked away from prying eyes but positioned for an unobstructed view of the entrance. Morozov's thumb drive hadn't provided a meeting time. That was fine; she could wait.

Kit settled into her seat, every sip of her dark coffee like a calculated chess move in a high-stakes game of double attack. Here she was, a lone queen on an undeclared battlefield, concealed within the ordinary setting of a morning cafe. The risks were a blend of bitter and aromatic, like her coffee, but essential to her strategy. Kit knew what was at play: unseen dangers lurking just beneath the surface, the way a bishop might hide behind a pawn. Now she waited— for Sergei, for the Vipers, for the next ghost from her past to make its move.

About fifteen minutes ticked by as patrons streamed in and out of the café, each leaving with their takeaway coffees cradled in hand. Nestled near the cash register, two varieties of cookies tempted the eye, and many succumbed, tucking a pair into brown paper bags as they went. Elsewhere, scattered individuals settled at tables, some lost in the day's news, others tapping away at laptops or absorbed in hushed phone conversations.

The doorbell chimed a deceivingly gentle tune, a stark contrast to the tension Kit felt. Sergei Sokolov made his entrance, the epitome of enigma. His stature was commanding, yet he moved with an understated grace. Wrapped in a shearling chocolate-brown jacket, its collar upturned against his neck, he donned aviator sunglasses that hid his eyes and any hint of his thoughts. Despite the casual air suggested by his fashionably unshaven face and the recent trim of his honey-brown hair, there was a deliberate precision in his step. He prowled through the space, a silent force, every movement echoing the stealth and focus of a predator.

A current of anxiety wound its way through Kit, her breath quivering on a precipice of lost composure. She kept her gaze anchored to her phone, thumb flicking past texts that held no meaning. Her coffee cup softly clinked, betraying the tremor in her grasp as she took a cautious sip, each swallow steeped in the potency of their shared past. Sergei was now with the rank of full colonel in Russia's military intelligence. Despite this impressive title, he remained to her an old flame, a man whose complexity was as alluring as it was dangerous.

Her peripheral vision captured Sergei scanning the café, vetting the faces. She sank deeper into her seat, trusting her scarf and sunglasses to camouflage her—a cover for her auburn locks and sky-blue eyes.

Her tension eased a notch when Sergei sat, mirroring her own position—back to the wall, full view of the cafe, hidden from the outside world. A coffee and an untouched newspaper sat in front of him.

Minutes later, the doorbell chimed again, signaling another entrant to the cafe. Her instincts flared. This man was different. If Sergei was a predatory feline, then this other man was a dangerous bear—formidable, muscled, and built to intimidate. With an imposing presence, he strode into the cafe, clad in a khaki padded jacket, cargo pants, and heavy boots. In his late forties, the man's face was framed by a grizzled beard, weathered but intense. It was the eyes, though—dark, almost coal-like—that grabbed her. They dissected the room, as if running real-time algorithms of risk and reward. Here was someone who combined raw muscle with a tactical mind. And for whatever reason, he was meeting Sergei.

Sergei rose, and the men shook hands. The newcomer sat down at the table. They began an intense conversation. Sergei's eyes narrowed as his companion spoke, a subtle change that Kit picked up. The lines around his mouth tightened, his posture subtly stiffened. For about fifteen minutes, the two men engaged in an intense, low-toned dialogue that Kit strained to overhear. At one point, Sergei scribbled something in a small notebook he had pulled from his pocket, tearing off a page and handing it to his burly counterpart. They exchanged nods, their faces serious, their eyes locked in a gravity that seemed to mute all other sounds in the café. Sergei punctuated the dialogue with brief sips of his coffee, the cup nearly empty now as the meeting concluded.

The men shook hands once more, a firm grip that carried an undercurrent of urgency. The heavyset man exited the café with the same air of restrained menace that he had arrived with, disappearing into the frigid morning.

Sergei sat back down, unfolded his newspaper as if he intended to read, but Kit saw the tension in his posture. He looked as though he was grappling with something, a decision perhaps. After a moment, he folded the paper, stood up, and walked toward Kit's table.

Her pulse spiked. Had he seen through her disguise? Kit's mind raced as Sergei closed the distance. As he moved closer, her pulse quickened. A thousand thoughts flashed through her mind. Had he recognized her? Was this a setup or another twist in this labyrinthine game? Kit felt adrenaline surge through her veins; every instinct screamed at her to be ready for anything.

"Ms. Chase," Sergei started. "You were the last person I expected to see here at *Kafja e Përfshtuar.*"

His tone of dry amusement made a grin tug at the corners of Kit's mouth. Memories flooded back—good times they'd shared, trust gained and then shattered, then rebuilt. The electric pull she felt when he was near prickled the hairs on her arms. She took off her sunglasses and motioned for him to join her.

"You look familiar. What's your name again?" she asked. She was aware of his tendency to use false identities, particularly when evading Interpol or undertaking covert operations. Although they were pretending not to know each other well, she was curious to know the truth.

"Oleg Sokora," he answered.

"Ah, the Ukrainian," she said, recalling that he used this name with a Ukrainian passport.

He nodded, signaling the barista, who, despite seeming disinterested, started brewing another cup of coffee.

"So, what brings you to town?" Kit probed. She wondered if he was linked to Morozov's murder. Poisoning was a Russian tradecraft hallmark. And his name was on that thumb drive.

"Just meeting an associate," he said.

"Congratulations are due, Colonel," she said, throwing him off balance by letting him know she had her own sources.

He didn't bite, accepting the coffee set before him by the barista. "Heard you visited Father Peter recently and talked about frequencies. Seems I introduced you to that concept some time ago."

That rattled her. How did he know about her meeting

with Father Peter? Unless the priest himself had been talking. She recalled their covert rendezvous in Bulgaria, where Sergei introduced her to frequencies and aromatherapy to deepen their connection. She felt her cheeks warm. Now it was her turn to be off balance.

"Yes, Father Peter and I had quite the enlightening conversation. Your name came up," Kit said.

"Did it now?" Sergei feigned surprise, his brow arching slightly.

She took a steadying breath. Their banter could go on, leading nowhere. She had to get her bearings and extract some benefit from this precarious situation. In hindsight, she realized she'd been naïve to think she could fool him with her rudimentary disguise. Sergei was a trained operative; he'd likely seen through her act from the moment he stepped into the cafe. As usual, rational thought seemed to evaporate when he was near, his magnetic presence derailing her. But she couldn't afford to let that happen again. She needed to maintain her edge, especially if she was going to unravel the web surrounding Morozov's death.

"Where do your superiors think you are right now?" he probed.

A twinge of unease ran through her, but she answered anyway. "They believe I'm picking up my cousin from the airport. She's flying in from New Zealand for the holidays. And I will. Her flight got delayed, so I had some time to kill."

His mouth twitched into a small, knowing smile. "And you thought you'd spend it here? How did you know I'd show up?"

Careful not to reveal too much, she said, "We're investigating a murder. Evidence suggested the victim might meet someone here this morning."

"So you staged a one-woman stakeout. Risky move, Ms. Chase," he said, savoring the last sip of his coffee. He was addressing her formally instead of using one of his pet names for her he used in their more intimate moments. She felt relieved by the way he was taking some distance from her. It helped her to keep up the appearance of a casual meeting.

"Sometimes, you have to gamble to win," she shot back, keeping her most valuable asset—the thumb drive—out of the conversation. "And what brings you here?" Kit asked.

"I just told you. Meeting an associate. He's given me some troubling news about Morozov," Sergei replied, a touch of disquiet in his eyes. Kit wondered if it was genuine. Sergei was a master at masking his true feelings.

"Who was that guy you met?" she pressed, curiosity piqued by the burly, bear-like man.

"That's need-to-know, and you don't need to know," he shot back.

"Give a little, get a little," Kit returned. "You're aware my organization is debating whether to revive that Interpol red notice for your activities in Staro Dorbi?"

His eyes flickered, the first sign of real unease. He scanned the café, eyes landing on the barista, who was busy polishing cups. "Alright, let's discuss this elsewhere. I'll text a location to your burner phone."

Sergei stood up, leaning in to kiss her cheek, a normal courtesy in Europe among associates. "Good to see you. We should catch up again soon."

His cologne enveloped her, and for a moment, her resolve wavered. She steadied herself against the table, nodding.

As he departed, she made her way to the counter and picked up some cookies for her cousin Paige. It was best they leave separately; the cookies would serve as a good diversion.

It was time to switch gears. Kit checked her watch; it was almost time to meet Paige. The flight from Vienna would land in the early afternoon. She got into her OIDC service vehicle and navigated her way to Pristina International Airport. As she drove, memories of her own arrival in Pristina flashed through her mind. She had come a long way since then, mentored by Angel and complicated by Sergei. He had been both a challenge and a paradox in her life— sometimes an enemy, sometimes a lover.

Her thoughts were interrupted as her jeep jolted over a pothole. She tightened her grip on the wheel, narrowly averting a collision with an oncoming car. She needed to stay sharp to avoid any missteps.

Upon reaching the airport and making her way to the arrivals zone, the arrivals board showed Paige's flight had already touched down. Kit's eyes darted across the sea of arrivals, her senses primed for any sign of Paige. Then she spotted her cousin: a figure embodying an adventurous spirit, a dynamo cutting through the crowd. Paige's sun-kissed blonde hair was pulled back in a casual ponytail, perfect for her on-the-go lifestyle. Her expressive blue eyes scanned the room with a thrill-seeking glint. She wore a youthful blend of sports attire—a fitted zip-up hoodie, sleek leggings, and a pair of sporty sneakers.

Paige's gaze met Kit's across the crowded concourse, and her face lit up. She barreled through the bustling sea of people, arms outstretched in anticipation. When they embraced their hug was like a balm on the wound of separation, a bright spot amidst the chaos of the terminal.

"Kit! It's so good to see you!" Paige's voice was filled with youthful excitement and anticipation.

"Welcome to Kosovo!" Kit replied, sensing her cousin's restless energy like a jolt to her system. "Ready for adventure?"

"Always," Paige fired back. For a moment, Kit wished that Paige's visit would be the uncomplicated, joyful interlude she so needed. Gazing into Paige's expectant eyes, she recognized that here, adventure was a double-edged sword.

Kit gestured toward the baggage claim, where passengers were crowding around the slowly spinning carousel. "Let's grab your bags and head out. Do you have everything you need for the European winter?"

Paige followed Kit, her eyes already darting around the room like she was taking mental snapshots. "Yeah, about that. I might've dropped the ball," she confessed. "I've been hitting the beach back in Auckland; can't really wrap my head around the whole winter thing."

Kit chuckled. "No worries, I've got you covered. There are jackets, hats, and snow boots available back at my apartment."

As they settled into Kit's service vehicle, Paige was a whirlwind of questions. "So what's it like working here? Is it as dangerous as it seems? Oh, and what about the food? And tell me about the murder investigation! You're investigating a murder, right?"

Focusing on the road as she juggled her cousin's inquiries, Kit felt as if she were balancing on a tightrope. "One question at a time, Paige. Yes, I'm on a case right now, and yes, it's not without its dangers. As for the food, you're in for a treat."

Upon arriving at the apartment, Kit had scarcely

crossed the threshold before she turned to Paige and asked, "Would you like a drink or something to eat?"

"Maybe later. I grabbed a bite on the flight," Paige said, vibrant with excitement. "So, what's the plan? I'm eager to get out and see everything!"

Kit smiled at her cousin's eagerness, but her thoughts edged toward the darker facets of her life in Kosovo. Paige sought adventure, yet in Kit's world, such escapades always bore consequences. Still, for the moment, she'd do her best to make sure her cousin's stay was as thrilling—and as safe—as possible.

"First thing, let's drop your bags. Then I'll introduce you to my team at the office, including a twenty-something intern who's offered to be your local guide. Plus, I've got a few adventures up my sleeve—Christmas markets, unique cafes, live music, you name it."

"Casinos?" Paige's eyes gleamed at the prospect.

"Nice try, but you're underage," Kit shot back. "There's plenty else though—museums, heritage sites, nature hikes. And you'll get to meet Owen, my boyfriend."

"Owen, Owen.. . . . Why does that name ring a bell? Refresh my memory.

What does he do?"

"He's a sergeant with the EUFOR military police, hails from Wales. Used to be a chef in Cardiff before he enlisted."

"Sweet." Paige grinned, clearly excited. "I can't wait to get the scoop on your Kosovo life. Lead the way, cuz."

"Get ready for a taste of it, at least," Kit said, tempering her cousin's enthusiasm with a touch of realism."

· · ·

As Kit pushed open the glass door of the OIDC office, a rush of air laced with the scent of pine and spiced apple greeted them. Angel Keys, the office assistant, perched on a stepladder, stringing lights along the walls. Across the room, French lawyer Axel Delcroix was steadying the base of a fir tree as German lawyer Christina Wacknagel strung it with tinsel and ornaments.

"In Germany, we have a precise way of decorating the tree," Christina said as she focused on the arrangement of ornaments. "First, the lights, then tinsel, followed by ornaments from largest to smallest as you go up. It's an art form."

Axel nodded, half-listening, his attention more on keeping the tree upright than on the details of German Christmas traditions. "*Oui, très intéressant.* Very interesting," he muttered.

"Ah, Kit, and you must be Paige," said Eva Refazo as she approached them, Bambino, her aging terrier, trailing behind her. "*Benvenute!*"

"Thanks, Eva! This is Paige, my cousin from New Zealand. Paige, this is my boss, Eva," Kit introduced them.

Paige greeted Eva, then her eyes immediately fell on Bambino. "And who's this little guy?"

"Bambino," Eva said, bending down to scoop the dog into her arms. "Rescued him over a year ago. He's become a bit of an office staple."

"Mind if I take him for walks sometimes?" Paige volunteered, her eyes twinkling. "I love dogs."

"I think Bambino just found a new friend," Eva laughed.

At last, they arrived at another desk where a young woman was bent intently over a stack of papers.

"Paige, this is Dua Rexhepi," Kit said. Dua looked up to

greet them with a radiant smile. "She's our intern from Albania. She has a law degree from the US."

As she tucked a strand of her glossy, black hair behind her ear, Dua exuded a vibrant spirit.

"Hey, great to meet you," Paige exclaimed, shaking Dua's hand. "Kit's told me you've offered to show me around?"

"Absolutely," Dua said. "There's a lot to see and do. You'll love it here."

Kit felt a wave of relief wash over her. Dua's offer to show Paige around town later not only relieved her from the duty but made her grateful that Paige would be in good company.

"Looks like you're all set," Kit told Paige, her eyes meeting her cousin's in a moment of mutual understanding.

"Trust me, I'm already excited." Paige grinned, her adventurous spirit already soaking in the energy of the place. "This is going to be fantastic."

"Come and see my office," Kit said, leading her along the corridor. "I'll ask Angela to organize a family pass for you so you can come and go more freely."

"Cool," Paige said.

Kit ushered Paige into her office, its window offering a view of the tree-lined compound outside. She gestured to the chair near her cluttered but organized desk overflowing with case files and legal documents. Paige took it all in, her eyes shining with unmasked excitement.

"So, this is where the magic happens," Paige broke the silence, glancing around. "I can't believe you're out there, making a real difference, Kit. I want to, too."

Kit eased into her own chair, her posture subtly tensing. "You're thinking about law school, then?"

"Yeah, I want to follow in your footsteps. Stand up for

those who can't speak for themselves, fight the good fight, you know?" Paige's eyes met hers, full of youthful enthusiasm.

Kit's heart swelled at her cousin's ambition, yet a knot tightened in her stomach. Memories of stressful nights fueled by caffeine, juggling cases in New Zealand, and facing the dangers of her current role flooded back to her. How could she guide Paige through the complexities of a life she was still figuring out herself?

Paige seemed to read the reservation in her eyes. "What is it? You think I can't handle it?"

"It's not that." Kit hesitated, searching for words. "It's rewarding, Paige, but also tough. And the international stage—well, it adds more complications. And sometimes, danger."

"So, what are you saying?" Paige prompted, her eyes narrowing.

Kit leaned back, eyeing the sports-themed keychain that dangled from Paige's backpack—a mini soccer ball. "You know, law school would mean less time for your soccer and all those outdoor activities you love."

Paige's eyebrows shot up, as if the thought had just crossed her mind. "Yeah, I guess there would be sacrifices."

"And not just time. Mental energy too. Law is all-consuming. It becomes your world," Kit said, thinking of nights when the glow of the computer replaced the moon-light on the beach, times when legal briefs edged out her gaming stats.

"Wow," Paige breathed out, her adventurous eyes clouding over for a moment. "You're making law school sound like an extreme sport."

"It is," Kit replied, a wry smile tugging at her lips. "It's a mental marathon, not a sprint. You'd have to be as committed to your studies as you are to landing a goal."

Paige chewed on her lip, contemplating. "If it's a marathon, then pacing is key, right? Balance."

"Exactly," Kit affirmed, warmed by her cousin's insight. "And if you decide to go down this path, maybe I can be your coach, or at least a mentor."

Paige's eyes lit up. "Deal," she said, her grin returning in full force.

Kit smiled back, but a sliver of caution remained. Life had taught her that even the best coaches couldn't shield players from every tackle.

There was a knock on the door. They looked up to see Dua grinning at the door, dressed in a coat, hat, and scarf, and carrying a shopping tote. "Ready for the best shops in Pristina and the Christmas market?"

Kit got up and handed Paige a spare winter jacket from the coat stand. "Dua will drop you back at my apartment when you've finished. Take your time, ladies." She smiled. Kit handed Paige a spare key for the apartment and a card with the address and her phone number written on it.

Kit's bag buzzed, a silent vibration that she'd grown to recognize as something apart from the typical pings of everyday life. With a last glance toward Paige and Dua, now engrossed in discussion as they prepared to leave, she unzipped the concealed pocket at the bottom of her bag. She pulled out a nondescript burner phone. The message from Sergei appeared from the burner phone's screen: "We need to talk. Choose a location: abandoned factory off Route 7, safe house near the old cathedral, or the private boat docked at Lake Badovc."

Kit's thumb hovered, suspended like her judgment. Each location promised privacy, yet offered its own form of exposure. Her mind toggled through mental snapshots of each venue, weighing their shadows and sightlines. The factory and the safe house? Conspicuous. Vulnerable to prying eyes. Lake Badovc's private boat offered natural isolation. A glance at her watch told her she had just enough time for the drive before dark. "Option 3," she replied.

Sergei's uncharacteristic offer of choices made her wonder. He seemed to be presenting the illusion of control, a tactic designed to heighten her feeling of security. Still, she remained acutely aware that comfort, much like control, was often a fragile illusion. With a heavy sigh, she stowed the burner phone back in its hiding place as the possible outcomes ran through her mind. Here she was, an encrypted message away from another clandestine meeting, a world apart from the youthful enthusiasm Paige exuded. Was this the life she would encourage her cousin to dive into? It was a question without an easy answer.

With that sobering thought, Kit resealed her bag and turned back to her desk. Her gaze briefly met Paige's from across the room, the younger woman waving energetically as she headed out. Kit forced a smile and waved back, feeling the contrast between their worlds deepen like a shadow at dusk.

Chapter 8

Boundaries and Chemistry

Kit glanced at her wristwatch as she walked briskly toward the car park. Thanks to Eva's flexible work schedule policy, she could drive out to Lake Badovc and make it back before Paige noticed she had ever left. She climbed into her four-wheel-drive service jeep, crucial for navigating the area's icy back roads. With GPS coordinates from Sergei guiding her, the drive from Pristina to Lake Badovc clocked just over thirty minutes. Exiting the city's major arterial route, she steered onto narrower roads, feeling the urban hum yield to nature's muted ranquility.

When Kit arrived, she got out of the jeep and brought her flashlight—this season, darkness rushed in quickly. She spotted the boat, moored tranquilly by the pier, and made her way toward it. Hidden in a secluded bay, the ship's dark hull seamlessly merged with the glossy, black surface, deterring any undesired attention.

Sergei appeared from the dark, hand outstretched. Kit took it, stepping onto the deck. A silent, shared isolation settled over them, thick as the oncoming night. Sergei's glance met hers in understanding.

"How was your drive? Did you tell anyone where you were headed?"

"The drive was okay," she said, dodging his second question. "But I'd like to return to Pristina before nightfall. These rural roads can turn treacherous quickly, and cell coverage is spotty."

She didn't voice the risks of their secret meeting—their isolation, the relentless march of time, her solo presence without backup. Tall pines and jutting rocks enclosed the space, giving the lakeside the air of a secluded fortress. On Lake Badovc, the boat became a private sanctuary, adrift from the chaos of their true worlds. Despite the urgency of their meeting, the pull between them was inescapable.

Inside the cabin, the decor was sparse: a table, chairs, a bench covered by a woolen rug, a radio, and a locker.

Sergei's presence was a force strong enough to eclipse Kit's mounting concerns. An electric charge filled the air, leaving her breathless. Memories of past meetings surged, vivid and intense. She relished the intoxicating bubble they'd stepped into but willed herself to keep sight of her objectives. Sergei's importance extended beyond his attraction. He held the key to her solving the Morozov murder and understanding the complex motives of the Black Sun and Siberian Vipers. And she needed to know: Where did he stand in this labyrinth of shifting alliances and veiled threats? Her pulse quickened, not just from the nearness of Sergei, but also from the precipice of revelations she sensed they were on the brink of.

"My cousin Paige's in town. An intern at the office is giving her the grand tour of Pristina. I can't be gone too long without raising eyebrows," she said.

"You have time," he said.

She took a moment to center herself before diving into her questions. "Morozov's murder. The intel suggests the Siberian Vipers and Black Sun may be involved. What do you know about them?"

"I'm aware of Black Sun's failed Halloween attack on your peacekeepers. Your team did well—two arrests, zero casualties."

A ripple of pride ran through her, but she kept her face neutral. "Who's your source?"

"I have my ways, as you do. Besides, we monitor the news reports. I can tell you the Siberian Vipers are trying to carve out a new Balkan route for their operations."

"I know that much. Got anything new for me?"

He stood, moving toward a cabinet. He slid open the rolling door, revealing an assortment of bottles. "Drink?"

She weighed the option. "Given I'm driving on sketchy roads after this, I'll pass. And I haven't forgotten Ljubljana. You spiked my drink."

"There were reasons," he said defensively. "You were never in real danger."

He turned, taking a sealed water bottle from the cabinet, twisting off the cap, and pouring it into a glass, all in plain sight. Then he poured himself a shot of vodka.

"That's debatable. But I'll stick with water. You haven't really answered me." She drew a heavy breath before continuing. "Sergei, enough with the games. We could go on like this forever. If you don't start giving me straight answers, I'm heading back to Pristina right now."

He sighed, studied his shot glass for a moment, and then downed the vodka. "You're right, Katarina." Using his private nickname for her signaled a shift in the conversation. "I'm on a covert GRU mission. Russian intelligence wants to curb the chaos that these criminals can create. I've been posing as a logistics consultant to Davor Nikolovski, the man you saw me with. He's ex-special operations, now a criminal entrepreneur, aiming to establish a new Balkan hub for trafficking—weapons, drugs, maybe even humans. His operation leverages existing criminal networks across Kosovo, Serbia, and Russia."

Kit muttered a curse. "Figures."

"The goods would likely move from Russia through Belarus and Ukraine, then into the Balkans via Hungary or Romania. They'd exploit corrupt officials in Serbia to get through to Kosovo. There is also the possibility of going through Bulgaria and North Macedonia, but it carries more risk."

"And the Siberian Vipers?"

"Middlemen. They help with the transit."

"What about the Black Sun?"

"Black Sun provides financial backing and has contacts that can ease customs and law enforcement barriers."

Kit tightened her grip on her glass, her knuckles whitening. "Those bastards tried to eliminate us. Probably to make this trafficking operation smoother. The foot soldiers probably didn't even understand why."

He nodded, pouring another shot of vodka. "Da, likely so."

"What about the leader of Black Sun? Someone known as 'Eclipse'?"

"That's part of what I'm trying to figure out. Whoever it is, they're adept at covering their tracks. My bet's on someone well-connected in Central or Western Europe," Sergei said.

Sergei locked eyes with her, his gaze unyielding. "Morozov was involved in the deals between the Vipers and

Black Sun, but as to who killed him, I'm as much in the dark as you are."

Kit bit her lip, holding back what she knew. Morozov had been a CIA informant. Someone had exposed him.

"Sergei, if they find out who you really are, you could be the next."

"I'm well aware, Katarina." He exhaled deeply. "It's part of the danger we sign up for. Changing gears, how's your khash training?" He switched topics so fluidly, it took her a moment to catch up.

"I'm still working with the frequency meditations Father Peter taught me," Kit responded. "The Tracer Fox has become more of a constant presence, but it can only guide me so far without solid leads. How about you?"

He took a moment, as if weighing what he should divulge. "I'm progressing, working on ways to fine-tune my intuitive skills. With what we're dealing with, any edge helps."

Sergei tossed back the vodka and poured himself another glass. The liquid shimmered under the boat's dim light. He glanced at Kit, who was holding her mineral water.

"To new beginnings," he said, lifting his glass.

"To justice," she replied, taking a sip.

Silence stretched between them for a moment. Finally, Kit leaned in closer, her voice softening. "Sergei, I know you have your own loyalties, your mission. I respect that. But this case—Morozov's murder—it happened on my turf. I have an obligation to find who did this and bring them to justice."

He looked at her, a hint of curiosity in his eyes. "You always did have a strong sense of duty."

"It's like a game of chess," she said. "Every move you

make, every piece you control, has consequences. It's all about strategy, but also about doing the right thing at the right time.

He smiled at the mention of the chess philosophy. "Khash teaches us to think multiple moves ahead, to see the bigger picture. Very fitting."

"Exactly," she continued. "We might be on different boards, playing different games, but right now our goals overlap. You want justice for Morozov too, don't you?"

He looked at her, a question in his eyes. "What's the play here?"

"Intel, Sergei. You're in places I can't be, hearing things that I can't. If you stumble onto something, you tell me. It would mean the world to me."

Sergei circled the vodka in his glass, weighing her suggestion. "You're cutting to the chase, I see."

She met his gaze, a smile playing on her lips at his pun on her name. "I learned it from you. So, do we have a deal?"

Their eyes met, a spark of old understanding igniting the air between them. "Fine. You'll have your updates, but on two conditions. My identity stays protected; the GRU won't tolerate any slipups, nor will I. That means I can't testify in court, ever. In return, be prepared to return the favor when the time comes."

Kit nodded. "With you, Sergei, there's always a trade-off."

He lifted his glass, a satisfied grin on his face. "To keeping the scales balanced then. And to justice."

As their glasses clinked, a jolt of tension dissipated from Kit's shoulders. She had secured the lifeline of intel from Sergei; a minor victory in a high-stakes game. Meeting his gaze, she felt a powerful attraction that disregarded their loyalties and social norms.

Kit felt a subtle shift, her mind easing into the moment. They couldn't go too far due to their world of secrecy, but they could still indulge in the chemistry between them. She shared deep understanding with Sergei, both of them guided by an intricate code that mixed ruthless practicality with an unyielding pursuit for justice. The power between them was tangible, electricity buzzing through their veins and hearts beating in time as desire took hold. The environment around them seemed to blur away. Their dance continued, the two of them aware of both the thrill and the fear of the unknown. It was a tenuous line they walked, fragile like a tightrope high in the sky above a cliff edge. But, in that instant, Kit realized that sometimes the greatest beauty lay in those moments of half-truths and unsaid words lingering in the air. And so they held onto it, cherishing what connected them and the vast possibilities ahead.

A palpable tension hung in the air as Kit and Sergei stood facing each other on the boat, their gazes locked in a silent standoff. A million questions seemed to hang in the precious moment between them. Did either of them have the courage to speak first? Kit felt her heart lurch as Sergei's hand slowly moved towards hers. When their fingers intertwined, it felt like every nerve ending was sizzling with anticipation. His touch was electric, sending jolts of desire through her body. The intensity of the pressure between them sent a wave of heat rolling up her spine. Her thoughts raced with a thousand possibilities. Did she dare to explore this forbidden attraction further? Could she afford not to?

Although neither of them spoke at that moment, Kit felt a new understanding pass between them. They had finally breached the walls of suspicion and protocol, allowing an unexpected intimacy to blossom. All traces of Owen,

Pristina, and the danger of their lives dissipated into a distant murmur. In that instant, all that mattered was what lay before them.

Eventually, they broke apart and gazed out across the lake, now almost completely cloaked in darkness. Without saying a word, Kit knew they shared an unspoken bond—a strength forged by secrets and strengthened by trust.

Later, as Kit navigated the icy roads leading back to Pristina, her mind raced faster than the jeep's engine. The headlights carved a path through the darkness, just as she was trying to carve a path through the intricate web of alliances and betrayals. Sergei's revelations echoed in her thoughts.

Could she trust Sergei enough to use him as a confidential informant? Doing so would place a huge amount of power in his hands, while also making him vulnerable. However, revealing his undercover status to her team would put his mission and their history at risk. Her gut churned at the thought.

The dilemma gnawed at her as the city lights of Pristina drew closer. Should she operate in the shadows, with Sergei as her secret asset? Or did her loyalty to her team and the mission demand full disclosure?

The skyline of Pristina emerged in the distance, each light leading her back but offering no illumination for the murky decisions that lay ahead. Kit gripped the steering wheel tighter. For now, she decided, she'd hold her cards close to her chest. After all, in a game where trust was a currency more valuable than gold, sometimes the best move was not to play your hand at all.

Kit stepped into her apartment, shrugging off her coat

along with the weight of the night and the secrets it held. The scent of pine and warmth enveloped her as she eyed the small Christmas tree, adorned with tinsel and baubles, standing in the corner of the living room. Paige and Dua were immersed in the festive spirit, giggling as they hung ornaments.

"You're late," Paige remarked, a teasing smile on her lips. "We had dinner without you. Where've you been?"

"Work stuff, you know how it is," Kit replied, her voice tinged with fatigue. Eager to shift focus, she asked, "So, how was your afternoon with Dua?"

Paige's face brightened. "It was amazing. The snow was so much fun! We hit up the Christmas market and even did some shopping. But"—her expression shifted—"some things took aback me. Kids begging on the streets, stray dogs. Dua showed me some bombed-out houses from the conflict too. It was eye-opening."

For a moment, Kit felt the sense of her own secrets intensify. Paige found herself in a world that was vastly different, yet she had barely scratched the surface. And there Kit was, sinking ever deeper into an underworld that could endanger them all. Her cousin's day of eye-opening experiences was a soft echo of her own, yet worlds apart. Kit stood on a precipice, torn between shielding Paige from the dangerous complexities of her life and pulling her into a reality she might not be ready to face.

The room closed in around her, the Christmas tree and its sparkling ornaments suddenly seemed like fragile baubles in a world fraught with peril. But for now, those dangers would have to wait.

"That's the reality here," Kit said softly. "It's a place of contrasts. Beautiful and broken at the same time."

As she spoke, Kit realized she could have been describing herself. Beautiful and broken, wrestling with decisions that could mend or shatter the lives hanging in the balance.

Dua looked up from the box of ornaments, her eyes meeting Kit's with a warmth that carried an undercurrent of quiet admiration. "I hope you don't mind the tree, Kit. Paige and I thought it would add a bit of holiday spirit. We had a great time at the Christmas market; it was buzzing."

Kit sensed that Dua knew there was a secretive and high-stakes world beyond the apartment, and she wanted to explore it. Dua was respectful enough not to probe, but her eagerness to be mentored by Kit was clear. She wanted to be part of Kit's circle of trust and showed it by being nurturing towards Paige.

Kit mustered a smile, pushing the lingering effects of her encounter with Sergei to the back of her mind. "I love it, thank you. It really warms up the space."

Dua's eyes twinkled with her next idea. "I was thinking, how about we take a trip to this women's collective I know? It's an empowering space, all about supporting local women. They make handicrafts, artisanal goods—completely self-managed. Could be good for Paige to see another side of Kosovo. Might even give you some holiday gift ideas."

The suggestion was innocent, well-meaning, but could she afford the distraction? Or was this moment of normalcy just what they needed? Because she had learned to expect the unexpected, Kit wondered if the women's collective would be the sanctuary they expected, or another layer of the labyrinth she was navigating.

"Sounds like a great idea," Kit finally said, putting her doubts aside, her eyes meeting Dua's. "Let's do it. Paige will love it, and so will I."

For tonight, the dangers would remain in the shadows, allowing a fragile peace to settle over the room, as delicate as the twinkling lights on their Christmas tree.

Chapter 9

The Gathering Storm

The next morning, Kit breezed into the office, Paige in tow. They carried bags of pastries from a local bakery, the aroma filling the air as they entered the break room. Staff perked up at the sight, eager for a morning sugar rush. Kit poured herself a coffee, conscious of the clock ticking toward a morning stacked with case files.

"What do you think about doing some Secret Santa shopping in town during lunch?" she asked Paige, who was chatting animatedly with a couple of team members.

"Yeah, and Dua said the women's collective is nearby. I'd love to see the handicrafts they're making. It's gotta be empowering and educational."

"Absolutely. Let's make it a plan."

Before Kit could escape to her sanctuary of files and focus, Owen walked in. "Got a minute, Kit?"

"Always. Owen, this is Paige, my cousin from New Zealand."

Instantly, Kit noticed them sizing each other up. Paige's

eyes lingered on Owen's military police uniform, a mix of curiosity and admiration in her gaze.

"Nice to meet you, Paige," Owen said, offering a handshake. "Heard you were visiting. Been looking forward to it."

"The feeling's mutual," Paige shot back, her grin infectious.

"We'd love to keep the holiday spirit going, but work keeps interfering," Owen remarked.

Right on cue, Dua intervened, inviting Paige to check out a project she was managing in the multimedia library. "It's about legal aid for local communities," she said, whisking Paige away.

Owen stepped into Kit's office, shutting the door behind him with a click. He was oblivious to her clandestine rendezvous with Sergei by the lake the night before or the emotional rollercoaster it induced. She needed some time to work through her inner battle soon, but for now, all her energy was focused on the task in front of her.

"I've got an update on our murder case," he said, his voice steady despite the brewing frustration. "Eyewitnesses identified two individuals near the murder site around the time of the murder. We've got names. But they've already fled to Serbia."

He paused, allowing the implications to sink in. The significance of the jurisdictional challenges hung in the air, a reminder of the legal and diplomatic tightrope they walked on. They knew all too well that cooperation with Serbia could be a slow dance, often just a formality. The undercurrent of politics between Kosovo and its neighbor—a reluctance to recognize Kosovo's independence—meant that extradition was a hope more than an expectation.

Kit's face tightened. "Out of our reach, but not invisible. Still, a dead end for now."

"A lead's a lead." Owen shrugged. "But it's not much."

Kit rubbed her temples, her mind racing. "We're missing pieces of this puzzle. Connections are there; we're just not seeing them."

"I've pitched a task force to Matt," Owen said, his face turning serious. "The Siberian Vipers, the tattoos, Black Sun—there's too much overlap to ignore. We need to throw more resources at this."

"Exactly," Kit agreed. "Black Sun's attack on EUFOR and OIDC could've been a dry run. What if they're aligning with other crime groups to expand operations?"

Owen scowled. "A joint venture in chaos. But it means we might need undercover intel."

Kit's eyes met Owen's. "Morozov was playing that role for the CIA. Look where it got him."

Owen exhaled, his gaze dropping to the desk. "Sorting this out is above my pay grade. Going undercover's not an option for us; we'd stick out like sore thumbs."

Kit chuckled. "Imagine that—my Kiwi twang and your Welsh lilt trying to go incognito."

Their laughter filled the room, a brief but necessary reprieve from the case. And for a moment, the vast, twisted landscape of their investigation felt a little less daunting.

The knock on the door came just as their laughter was subsiding. Kit swung it open to reveal Angel, clutching her ever-present planner and pen. "Didn't mean to crash the party," Angel said, her Yorkshire accent bright and clear. "But Eva's called for a meeting. The boss upstairs is eager for an update on the case, and there's someone new to introduce to the team."

"New staff? Not sure throwing them into this firestorm is the best idea," Kit said, a frown lining her face.

"Name's Katya Petrova," Angel continued. "She's joining the executive office and will coordinate on a range of issues, including this case."

"Where's she from?" Kit's senses tingled, throwing up red flags.

"Couldn't tell you." Angel shrugged. "I just deliver the messages. Eva also said Owen should come along. You know, for the EUFOR angle."

Owen stood, producing his phone. "I didn't plan for a morning meeting, but if it's necessary, I'll attend. I should check with Matt first, though."

"No need," Angel interjected. "Eva already got the green light from Major Hackman."

Kit felt her internal alarms sounding, but she quashed them—for now. With a nod, she saw Angel and Owen out, her mind racing ahead to the meeting.

Within the hour, Kit was navigating the familiar corridors leading to Bo Westergaard's office, now the head of the OIDC. His workspace was as large as his reputation, and she was becoming well-acquainted with its imposing door and the spacious room beyond.

As Kit stepped inside, Westergaard rose from his chair. His stature was not imposing, yet he carried an air of unmistakable authority. The silver in his hair glinted under the office lights, a striking contrast to his weather-beaten features—evidence of a life shaped by fieldwork rather than desk jobs. Though his years were apparent, there was an undeniable sprightliness in his movements. His voice when he spoke, textured and deep, filled the room.

This time, the cast had expanded: Eva, her direct superior; Owen Reese, representing EUFOR; and a fresh addition—Katya Petrova, a young Russian woman who radiated a calculated allure. Standing a couple of centimeters taller than Kit, her light brown hair flowed in waves down her back, and her face held a practiced warmth that didn't quite reach her eyes. She wore a mid-thigh skirt, revealing just enough skin to intrigue while maintaining an air of professionalism. A silk blouse completed the ensemble, adding a touch of elegance. Her jewelry was discrete, a dainty gold chain around her neck and matching earrings. Kit's internal alarm continued its low-frequency hum; this woman was not to be underestimated.

"Please, have a seat. Coffee?" Westergaard's gravelly voice broke Kit's chain of thought. He extended a hand toward the cream leather couches that populated his office. It was an offer Kit had learned to appreciate, a small mercy in a world of chaos.

"Thank you, yes," Eva said, taking the lead as Kit and Owen echoed her sentiment. Westergaard's assistant took their orders and exited the room with a fluid grace that spoke of quiet efficiency.

Brad Harris, Westergaard's right-hand man, was as sharp and sophisticated as Kit remembered. He exchanged a brief nod with Katya.

The office was a high-level sanctuary tinged with cultural flair, local artwork lending splashes of color to its otherwise muted tones. But today, an air of tension undercut the room's usual tranquility.

As Kit cradled the hot cup of coffee, its steamy aroma providing a momentary distraction, she became keenly aware that they weren't just here for a status update.

"So," Westergaard began, his eyes sharp and probing, "let's get down to business. We have newcomers and returning faces in this room, all of whom are crucial to the case at hand. Let's discuss the findings from the murder site and how we're going to proceed."

Owen shifted in his seat, eyeing Katya as if sizing up a potential opponent. Kit looked at Eva, who gave her a subtle nod. The floor was hers, but as she spoke, she couldn't shake the feeling that Katya was a wild card that could either break or make their entire operation.

Kit took a moment to organize her thoughts, her eyes briefly flicking to Katya before settling on Bo Westergaard and Eva. "Thank you for having us, sir," she began, taking a sip of her coffee for fortitude. "The discovery of cryptic text on the murder victim at the Christmas market has made our investigation more pressing. The murder of Anatoly Morozov is troubling for several reasons."

Clearing her throat, she continued, "EUFOR had a team survey the surrounding areas. Eyewitness accounts helped us identify two persons of interest. But the unfortunate news is that these individuals appear to have left Kosovo for Serbia. We are liaising with Serbian authorities, but our jurisdiction is limited there."

Owen interjected, "EUFOR is equally concerned about possible links to two factions—the Siberian Vipers and the Black Sun group, whose symbols were inked on the deceased. Given the latter's recent activities, this connection can't be overlooked."

"That sure is a volatile mix. And you say these messages were inked onto the body?" Brad Harris asked.

"Yes, a troubling signature," Kit replied, holding back the specifics of what the inked messages actually said. She shifted her gaze to Katya briefly before focusing back on Westergaard. "There's a likelihood of an expanding conspiracy involving multiple criminal groups. We're considering involving undercover agents to delve deeper."

"Are there any motivations you're exploring?" Westergaard asked.

"We're looking into several angles, including rivalries among crime syndicates and financial or political motivations. But it's still early days," Kit said cautiously.

"Thank you for the update, Kit," Westergaard concluded. "We'll provide all the support we can to ensure the success of this investigation."

The alarm in Kit's head persisted. She felt like she was playing chess with an unseen opponent, each move pregnant with hidden dangers.

Brad Harris raised an eyebrow, noting Kit's recurring presence at key events. "You thwarted the Black Sun attack on EUFOR and OIDC during Halloween, and now you're among the first on the murder scene. An intriguing pattern, wouldn't you say?"

Resisting the urge to retort with sarcasm, Kit answered, "I can't explain the coincidence, sir."

"May we have copies of all relevant reports? Coroner's findings, crime scene investigations, witness interviews?" Katya said.

Kit's eyes darted to Eva, her thoughts echoing in the room's tense silence. Sharing the identities of their witnesses, even within the organization, could place them in grave danger, susceptible to coercion or worse.

Eva stepped in. "We can make available a summary of the case, but full access to specific reports may be restricted because of a pending court order. Isn't that correct, Kit?"

Kit caught Eva's cue like a pro. "Exactly. We have a court hearing set. We can't undermine that process by sharing sensitive details prematurely."

Westergaard glanced at his organizer, aware that time was passing. "Alright, I have no intention of stepping on judicial toes. It's important that you keep us in the loop as much as possible. Got it?"

"Absolutely, sir," Kit responded, intentionally avoiding eye contact with Katya. She felt the room's tension dissipate as Westergaard seemed eager to wrap things up. Kit allowed herself a mental sigh of relief; they'd navigated another tight spot, at least for now.

Owen hit the elevator for the car park, linking up with Matt Hackman for an officers' meeting, while Eva and Kit took the stairs back to Eva's office.

"I get that you're not a fan of Katya, Kit. But optics matter; we need to at least seem to be on the same team," Eva said.

"Her credentials puzzle me. She seems green for an executive office job," Kit said.

"Probably has a contact in high places," Eva speculated. "After that Russian liaison fiasco with the Staro Dorbi murders, her sudden appearance here makes me uneasy. But remember, OIDC is a global operation. Keep friends close, enemies closer."

Kit's mind shifted toward Sergei, a connection she wanted to keep under wraps. "Exactly," she said, keen to change the subject. "Speaking of, I'm planning to take Paige and Dua shopping during lunch. Dua wants to introduce Paige to the Women's Craft Collective."

"Nice. Paige is a gem, you know. She really looks up to you," Eva said.

"I'm not sure I'm such a great role model," Kit replied, half-joking.

"Don't sell yourself short. You're a cornerstone of this office."

Kit smirked. "We'll see about that. Stars can plummet too."

"Before you head out, please make a file note of that meeting. I want a clear record of case discussions. Let's limit what leaves this room and cover our tracks if something slips."

"Already on it," Kit said. "More lives could be on the line. I'll start on the court filing as well. I suspect this murder is just the tip of the iceberg. We saw the deadly intentions of the Black Sun at Halloween. Teamed up with the Siberian Vipers, who knows what havoc they could cause."

"Agreed. That angle about the court filing was a spur-of-the-moment idea, but it should keep the brass at bay," Eva said.

"And keep Ms. Katya Petrova out of things that are not her concern."

Back in her office, Kit fished out her burner phone from her bag. It was time to put her new arrangement with Sergei to the test.

"Know anything about Katya Petrova? Just started here."

Moments later, a chilling reply came back: "FSB."

Kit's finger hovered over the screen, pausing at Sergei's three-letter text—FSB. Her stomach tightened. She glanced around her office, the walls closing in like they knew some state secret. FSB and GRU, she thought—two Russian intelligence agencies, both predators in the same jungle but rarely sharing a kill.

The Federal Security Service of the Russian Federation, also known as the FSB, served as Russia's primary security agency. Its responsibilities encompassed internal security, counterintelligence, and surveillance. Widely regarded as the heir to the infamous Cold War-era agency, the KGB, the FSB held significant influence. On the other hand, the Main Directorate of the General Staff of the Armed Forces, or the GRU, operated as Russia's military intelligence service. The GRU's role in safeguarding national interests involved tasks like espionage and cyber warfare.

Sergei, her GRU contact, had an edge, a shadow in his eyes when he spoke of home. Katya, if she was FSB, wore a different mask. One that smiled in the hallways and stabbed in the dark. Kit wondered if Sergei and Katya's agendas collided or aligned. Either way, she felt like the wire in a ticking time bomb. One false move and she'd set off an inter-agency Russian war.

Chapter 10

Into the Abyss

The women's collective market was a lively and enchanting blend of colors, sounds, and scents. The venue was adorned with twinkling lights, making handmade trinkets and artisan goods look magical. Laughter rang out as women tried on vibrant scarves and haggled over handcrafted jewelry.

Kit, Paige, and Dua wove through the crowds, a sense of collective effervescence lifting their spirits. For Kit, the market provided a temporary respite from the grueling demands of her work, a place to immerse herself in the ordinary joys of the season.

Amidst the array of wares, Kit's eyes settled on an unpolished Trepča crystal. Its natural beauty was captivating—a cluster of quartz sprinkled with golden flecks, untouched but mesmerizing in its raw state. She considered it for a moment as a Secret Santa gift, appreciating how its rough elegance paralleled the complexities of her own existence. Mined from the depths of Trepča, it was a hidden treasure of Kosovo.

Just as she was contemplating a handcrafted rug,

vibrant with intricate designs, her gaze drifted. A large mirror framed by fairy lights captured her attention. The mirror reflected the market's bustling activity, but among the faces, she saw him—Sergei. Dressed in disguise, his hat low over his forehead, it was undeniably him. Their eyes met in the reflection, and a slight nod from Sergei directed her towards a less crowded corner.

The atmosphere shifted perceptibly. Holiday warmth receded, replaced by a jolt of adrenaline. With that fleeting glance, the festive backdrop mutated. It was no longer a haven of festivity but more like a chessboard, every piece positioned for a critical play.

She turned to Dua and Paige. "I need a moment," she murmured as she moved away to the space that Sergei had indicated.

Dua met Kit's eyes, her gaze lingering for a fraction of a second longer than normal. There was an understanding in that look that signaled Dua's awareness of the high-stakes world Kit navigated. Though keen to learn and eager to be part of Kit's inner circle, Dua had the savvy to know when to keep quiet. She returned to the table of handcrafted gifts.

Paige's sidelong glances caught the silent exchange of electricity in the air between Kit and Sergei. Paige, ever the aspiring lawyer at seventeen, believed in dissecting undercurrents, thinking they were the keys to sophistication. Sergei, with his enigmatic presence, seemed like a puzzle she was itching to solve.

As Sergei stepped away, Paige couldn't shake off the pull of the hidden forces at play. She trailed after Sergei, drawn into the web of secrecy that Kit knew all too well. The market's festivity receded into the background, overshadowed by the unfolding drama. Following Sergei, the sheltered comforts of Paige's life in New Zealand seemed galaxies away, replaced by this pulsating energy of a world she knew so little about. Her heart raced with naïve excitement, each step down this dangerous path validating her sense of adventure. Somewhere in the back of her mind, the assurance lingered that Kit, her indomitable cousin, would be her safety net. With that reassuring thought as her anchor, Paige pushed forward.

In the murky light that draped Pristina's forgotten backstreets, Paige's grip on her phone was vice-like, the camera app ready, her thumb lingering over the record button. Her pulse hammered a frantic rhythm, mirroring the gravity of trailing Sergei into this den of shadows. As Sergei confronted a burly figure, whose menacing aura chilled the night air, Paige's breath stilled, and she hit "record." The two men swept cautious glances around before Sergei, with calculated movements, exchanged a small, brown parcel with the intimidating stranger, who concealed it within his jacket.

Her eyes widened as she spotted a cryptic tattoo peeking from beneath the man's rolled-up sleeve. She couldn't quite put her finger on it, the black circle with its twisted arms gave off a cult-like vibe that she couldn't ignore. A chill seized her as she stared at the scene she had stumbled upon. Awareness dawned—she was treading dangerous waters that could swallow her whole. The realization pressed upon her lungs, a suffocating truth, yet retreat was no longer an option.

The piercing chime of a low-battery alert emanating loudly from her phone shattered the tense quiet. Paige's eyes widened in horror. Across the alley, Sergei's head snapped up, his gaze becoming more focused as they scanned the darkness. They had seen her. The heavy, sinking feeling in her stomach told her she was a glaring liability.

Nikolovski, a man whose presence oozed menace, seemed to get a signal from somewhere. His eyes shifted, locking onto the shadows where Paige hid. Her heart raced as adrenaline coursed through her body.

Frantic, Paige pocketed the phone and turned to flee, but her boots barely scraped the cobblestone before she was yanked backward. A hand clamped over her mouth, another seizing her arm in a vice-like grip. Panic clawed at her insides, every thought obliterated by the realization that she was being pulled into the very web of criminal intrigue she'd dared to spy on. Her aspirations for law school, her naive confidence—shattered in an instant, as the dark world she'd glimpsed swallowed her whole.

Sergei's eyes meet Nikolovski's in a silent exchange tense with unspoken questions. Sergei's hands were empty, the small package he delivered now in Nikolovski's possession. Faced with a damning choice, Sergei calculated the risks. To act was to endanger his year-long undercover mission; to remain quiet was to place the young woman he had seen with Kit, presumably the cousin she had spoken of, in immediate peril.

Nikolovski signaled to one of his henchmen, who swiftly moved to gag Paige with a dirty kerchief, silencing any attempt at speech or scream. Her gaze darted toward Sergei, locking onto his for a split second. The tiniest of head shakes from him told her all she needed to understand —stay silent. The question loomed: Could he, would he intervene? Or was she merely a pawn in a dangerous game, her life a risk he had already calculated and accepted?

Nikolovski snatched Paige's phone from her pocket,

eyes narrowing as he skimmed through the incriminating footage.

"What's the plan?" Sergei spoke without emotion.

"Tomorrow's meeting is too important to be jeopardized. The high-stakes rendezvous with representatives from Black Sun and the Siberian Vipers in our Accursed Mountains stronghold." Nikolovski's words dripped with venom. "We can't afford disruptions. Take her to headquarters. We'll figure out how much she knows."

The henchman shoved Paige, now bound, further inside the van. Nikolovski shot her one last glance before slamming the doors shut, and the engine started.

By the time Kit returned to Dua, the crowd blurred into a sea of faces. No Paige in sight. "Where's Paige?" Her voice frayed at the edges, tinged with a raw urgency. Her stomach clenched, escalating the knot of panic.

"She followed that guy you were talking to," Dua said.

"Why didn't you stop her?" Kit almost shouted, her disbelief mingling with a rising fury.

"I didn't think she'd actually keep going," Dua stated defensively.

Kit's heart hammered against her rib cage. Her fists tightened, knuckles pale and strained. "That's the group tied to the murder case we've been investigating. We have to find her. Now."

She frenetically assembled a plan to find Paige. Mistakes had been made, but there was no time for regret. Now, it was a race to pull Paige back from the precipice she'd unwittingly stumbled upon.

Chapter 11

The Ticking Clock

Kit's boots pounded against the streets, her breath short, as she and Dua split up to search the area around the marketplace. Her burner phone buzzed in her bag. Sergei's encrypted ID flashed on the screen. Her thumb hesitated for a split second before answering.

"Talk to me," she growled.

"Nikolovski has the young woman you were with. I presume she's the cousin you spoke of. They caught her filming our meeting." Sergei's voice cut through, icy but with an undercurrent of urgency. "They're taking her to the base in the Accursed Mountains."

The words slammed into her like a blow to her gut. Her mind sketched an image of Paige, restrained and terrified.

"A high-level meeting with Siberian Vipers and Black Sun is set for tomorrow," he said, his words sinking her further into a well of fear. "You need to retrieve her before it concludes."

Anger welled up, mingling with her surging adrenaline. "Why didn't you stop them?"

"Doing so would have blown my cover. Besides, I couldn't. His armed security caught her filming us with her phone. That puts us both at risk."

"What will they do to her?" Her voice trembled on the brink of breaking.

"If she's lucky . . ." Sergei paused, weighing his words. "She'll end up being trafficked."

The world blurred, narrowing to the immediacy of Sergei's words. "We have limited time, then."

"Agreed," Sergei said.

"Do you have the location of their base in the mountains?"

Sergei messaged her the GPS coordinates.

The call ended, leaving Kit standing freezing in the winter air, her breaths coming in visible puffs. She had to craft a story, a smoke screen to protect both Paige and Sergei. Her mind raced, formulating plans, then discarding them. There was no room for error. Time was evaporating, leaving her with a narrowing list of hellish choices. She couldn't face telling her family that something bad had happened to Paige. She had to find her cousin before that became necessary.

Kit snapped the phone shut, strategies whirling in her mind. The task ahead was to feed Eva and Owen a convincing narrative—one that omitted Sergei's true role in all this. Her focus sharpened, walking this informational tightrope. Eva had a prosecutor's eye for discrepancies. She'd demand the who, the what, the why. Seconds hung heavy as Kit weighed her words, teetering on the precipice of a critical gamble.

First, Eva. Kit initiated the call.

"*Pronto*," Eva answered in Italian.

"Eva, it's Kit. Something terrible has happened. Paige is

in the hands of the organized crime group responsible for the Morozov murder." Kit pushed the words through a clenched jaw.

Eva inhaled sharply. "*Mia madre.* How? You were supposed to be shopping!"

"A new informant approached me at the market. He said he had intel on a high-stakes meeting with Black Sun and the Siberian Vipers tomorrow in the Accursed Mountains. Wanted to keep things below the radar, out of the office," Kit said, each word a tightrope step. "Paige saw us, followed him, and now she's been caught. The informant's cover is probably blown now, and we're racing against the clock."

The words left her lips smoothly, a risky subterfuge underpinned by nuggets of truth. "We need to act fast."

"If you know their location, we can get Paige back," Eva insisted. "I'll contact Major Hackman for a tactical team. Meet back at the office."

"Yes, the CI gave me the location before he disappeared."

Dial tone. Kit inhaled a shaky breath, eyes locking with Dua's concerned gaze.

"What now?" Dua queried.

"We're meeting Hackman about sending a rescue mission. The clock's ticking, but we could nail this syndicate while getting Paige back," Kit affirmed, taut with resolve.

Dua nodded.

"One more thing. Let me handle the explanation for this afternoon," Kit added. She couldn't afford another chink in her rapidly constructed version of events. There were too many variables, too many things that could go gut-wrenchingly wrong. But there was no other play.

Chapter 12

On the Edge

The EUFOR Operational Center was a hum of efficiency, screens flickering with satellite images and real-time intel. A mixture of muted typing and murmured radio conversations filled the air as the EUFOR flag—a star-spangled constellation on a blue background—anchored the middle of the room. This was the symbol of Europe's unified force. Major Matt Hackman, his green eyes commanding attention, sat at the head of a glossy black conference table. Hackman's intense gaze was the focus for everyone in the room. His hardened cheeks and slightly crooked nose were a testament to all he had seen and endured.

Kit sat next to Owen Reese, her source of strength in a difficult world. She was dressed practically from head to toe —a black roll-neck top, tactical pants, and hiking boots—the stress registered on her pale face. Across from her was Eva, carefully studying the dossier in front of her, hunting for secrets. The remaining seats around the table were filled with a variety of military professionals, each an expert in their field. One of these was Don Edgson, a tall Texan who headed the Canine Unit team. His faithful Tervuran dog, Max, lay at his feet, ears perked attentively.

Hackman spread out a satellite map of the Accursed Mountains and stated, "Our first priority is to find Paige White and extract her." Owen displayed a beachside photo of her, looking so young and innocent it made Kit's heart ache. He continued, "Secondary target is our assumed OCG leader who intel has identified as Davor Nikolovski. His hideout—Iron Hub—is located in the Accursed Mountains. Aptly named," he added with a dry smile. "We need to track down evidence on the Black Sun and Siberian Vipers—two criminal organizations with different motives, but united by money. Morozov's intel pointed at the involvement of both gangs. If we move quickly enough, we may even uncover proof to link them to Morozov's murder."

Owen displayed a satellite map of Nikolovski's isolated base—complete with access roads, outhouses, and a helipad.

"We have to be ready to go in two hours before dawn on December twenty-third," Hackman announced. He explained the plan: Alpha team would be inserted by helicopter near the entrance to the base, which included Don and his canine unit. Ground team Bravo—with Kit and Dua playing support roles—would go in under the darkness of night, leaving their vehicles well away from the gate.

Eva spread out a variety of photos and documents. "Our information confirms that Black Sun is involved in serious criminal activity, including terrorism. We need undeniable proof of their crimes for prosecution."

"I must be there, not just for Paige but also for the accuracy of the evidence collected," Kit said.

Dua leaned in closer to the group, dressed in camo

pants and a khaki sweater. "My responsibility for Paige's situation makes me want to join you all for this mission as well. I can support Kit and also be useful to extract data from the servers. I studied data forensics as part of my legal studies. "

Eva frowned in concern. "Don't forget that you both are lawyers, not field agent."

Kit glanced at Hackman before responding. "I'd never forgive myself if I didn't do something to get Paige back. Please, Eva. I can't be responsible for ruining all my families Christmases going forward by losing my cousin."

Finally, Eva inclined her head. "Alright. You've shown you can handle yourself in the field. But let the record show that I warned against it."

Hackman's gaze swept over the group before him, his eyes silently conveying something to each of them. "We have less than a day. Any thoughts?"

Kit was about to answer when the door opened and Katya Petrova stepped in, looking as if she had just come from the head office. She walked towards an empty chair near the front of the room and gave them an enigmatic smile.

"I'm here on behalf of the deputy head of mission at OIDC," she said. "It's important that senior management stays in the loop."

Kit felt her grip tighten around her folder; remembering Sergei's advice. It was obvious now that Katya had been sent by Moscow for intelligence-gathering.

Eva spoke up quickly. "Thank you for your offer, Ms. Petrova, but I will inform both the head of mission and chief of staff directly myself."

Katya smiled again—a sharp smirk this time—and

reached into her bag to get her notepad. "I am only following orders from those higher up," she said.

Major Hackman glanced at Katya before directing his glance between Kit and Eva. "Thanks for joining us—we were just finishing up. I'll leave it to the prosecutor's office to coordinate with the executive office of OIDC. Time is ticking. Be ready to move two hours before dawn."

Kit resisted the urge to imagine worst-case scenarios with her colleagues about Paige's fate as the afternoon light filled the office. She felt a tug within her, as if the meditations Father Peter had provided were given for this very moment. Driven by a relentless urge to find an upper hand against the merciless figure who'd abducted Paige, Kit decided to head back to her apartment. Her sanctuary now became a place to hone her focus, sharpen her strategy. To avoid unwanted calls from New Zealand about Christmas plans, she switched off her regular phone and kept her burner phone active. If Sergei had last-minute intel, she needed to hear it. The device lay silent, though.

She sank into her couch, savoring the warmth of her cup of tea against her palms. Her fingers unfurled Father Peter's note page, revealing the neat, handwritten words. "Custom-made," he had promised.

Meditation: "The battle belongs to the Lord, and he will deliver all of you into our hands" (1 Samuel 17:47).
Chess: The Strategy for Underdogs.
khash Element: Tracer Fox.
Frequency: 528 Hz.

· · ·

She felt like a modern-day David, small yet resolute, confronting a colossal criminal Goliath. Retrieving Natalia's frequency amplifier from a cupboard, Kit adjusted it to 528 Hz.

"I need one of these," she thought as the apartment filled with a sonic landscape around that specific frequency. With each beat of the music, her fears for Paige surged, transforming into a concentrated energy that awakened her inner Tracer Fox—resourceful, elusive, and instinctive. The liminal hours before dawn were approaching; twilight times when her metaphorical fox—and her resolve—would be at its peak.

As she pondered over the verses of 1 Samuel 17, they resonated within her, creating gentle ripples of understanding. Although she didn't consider herself religious, she would grasp any advantage divine intervention might offer. As her mind shifted gears, she became aware of her surroundings, her senses tingling with a predator-like intensity.

Then it came—a prickly sensation that tingled at the edges of her awareness. It refused to be ignored. Yielding to the instinct, her thoughts darted to the flash drive locked in her safe. She hadn't given it much thought since its concealment, but now, propelled by a gut sensation she couldn't deny, she rose to retrieve it. Maybe, just maybe, it held some hidden advantage for the dawn raid in the Accursed Mountains.

Kit's laptop hummed to life as she snapped the thumb drive in. The chaotic jumble of events—Sergei's unexpected appearance, Paige vanishing—had kept her from fully examining its contents. Her eyes zeroed in on Sergei's appointment that had led her to him. A split-second decision, a click of the finger, and the reference to Sergei vanished into digital oblivion. With an operation this covert, the less known about Sergei—and her connection to him—the better. But otherwise, the drive was a gold mine—financial records that could tighten the noose around Mueller.

A fabricated tale about her mysterious informant slipping the drive into her pocket at the market would have to suffice as an explanation for others. But now she needed more. While skimming the files, she found the jackpot—a detailed plan of Davor Nikolovski's lair, including entry and exit points, and power sources. Morozov's death hadn't been in vain

Kit's fingers hovered over the keyboard, combing for Sergei Sokolov's name. She found a fleeting mention and erased it. She knew she was skating on thin ice. Tampering with evidence was a serious offense. But she gambled that her digital tracks would blur into obscurity among the welter of entries. Satisfied, she fired off a text to Eva attaching the schematics of the Iron Hub. This intel was too volatile to sit idle. Her phone vibrated almost instantly with Eva's reply: Owen was already on his way. The thumb drive's data was slated for immediate forensic scrutiny.

Leaning back on the comfortable sofa and sipping her now lukewarm tea, Kit felt a surge of hope flood her for the first time since discovering that corpse days ago. The weight of knowing she had concealed the thumb drive lifted. It had served its purpose for her, and now it was time to pass it on.

A short time later, Owen materialized at her doorstep with the blend of urgency and personal history. A quick, meaningful hug was exchanged—no time for more. She handed him the thumb drive, which he promptly sealed into an evidence bag, scribbling a label.

"Keep Katya's hands off this. I don't trust her as far as I can throw her," Kit warned.

Owen nodded curtly. "I'm taking this to forensics. If it holds what we think it does, it's gold." He glanced at his watch, a note of concern filtering through. "Try to grab some shut-eye. I'll be back at zero five hundred to pick you up."

Chapter 13

The Iron Hub Summit

Tucked into the craggy folds of the Accursed Mountains, the Iron Hub base was the dark heart of Davor Nikolovski's empire. Just two hours from Pristina, it combined tactical brilliance with luxurious living. Being strategically positioned in Kosovo and close to Albania and North Macedonia, it served as the perfect focal point for criminal operations, facilitating the import-export of illegal commodities ranging from drugs and firearms to human cargo.

The Iron Hub, with its fortified design, was an architectural feat. It seemed to melt into the rocky terrain, its levels descending along the mountain face. Like a predator in its lair, the complex was all but invisible at a distance to the untrained eye, shielded by dense pine forests and towering cliffs.

Encased in an electrified fence, the Iron Hub left little to chance. Well-armed guards patrolled the perimeter from lookout posts elevated for a bird's-eye view as CCTV cameras swept the area. A helipad sat ready for VIP arrivals, typically members of the criminal elite, who arrived and left discreetly. A solitary, serpentine road cut its way through the jagged terrain, providing the only way in or out. The risk of landslides was another layer of security through enforced isolation.

Next to the estate, a modern weapons range disrupted the tranquility with the rapid fire of live rounds. Nikolovski's mercenaries sharpened their aim here, becoming more precise with deadly instruments. The Iron Hub was an impenetrable fortress, a covert operations center, and a monument to the aspirations of its owner, Davor Nikolovski.

As evening fell, the Iron Hub came alive with luxury SUVs snaking their way up the treacherous road, their headlights dancing across the jagged cliffs. Stealth helicopters, their blades nearly silent, touched down on the helipad. A group of dangerous underworld figures emerged, including warlords, black-market leaders, and corrupt politicians.

The reception area, a shadowy and opulent enclave, housed a towering Christmas tree that flickered in the corner, its lights providing an ironically festive touch. Festive strings of LED bulbs framed the windows, casting a surreal glow on the gathering. Lena Markovic, Davor's half-sister, was the epitome of grace under pressure. She effortlessly served champagne and hors d'oeuvres, skilled in both social graces and subterfuge. With her expertise as a journalist, she was skilled at working a room, making people feel at ease, and eliciting their secrets. As a Black Sun group operative, she knew how to keep their clandestine goals front and foremost in her mind.

Davor Nikolovski held court at the center of the space. Tonight, the dangerous bear of a man had traded his military gear for a tailored black suit, yet the aura of menace was unmistakable. He scanned the room, calculating the dynamics of the assembly before him. He greeted the member of the Siberian Vipers, Igor Kuznetov, with a hug that belied the deadly intentions they both harbored.

Just as Davor raised his glass for a toast, one of his lieutenants inclined his head towards him, whispering in his ear. "The girl has been secured, sir."

A wave of annoyance crossed Davor's face. Under any other circumstances, he would have dropped everything to interrogate this new catch, but tonight, priorities shifted. This event was his majestic reveal—a demonstration of a revolutionary partnership between his own operations, the Siberian Vipers, and the Black Sun, orchestrated to convince the other players.

"Very well," he responded, his voice a low growl. "Keep her isolated. Give her some food and water. I don't want her collapsing before I've finished with her. I'll deal with her after we've wrapped things up here."

His eyes met Lena's across the room. A silent communication passed between them, a shared understanding of the importance this night held. The air was thick with tension, and yet, for just a moment, it was as if they both allowed themselves a fleeting sense of triumph. Their network was growing, extending its dark tendrils across borders and underworld markets. And this was just the beginning.

Davor Nikolovski went to the front of the elegantly decorated reception area. He cleared his throat, his gravelly voice silencing the chatter among the guests—twenty in total, all formidable figures in the criminal underworld. In his fitted suit, he radiated threat, his bearlike physique dominating the space.

"Ladies and gentlemen," he began, scanning the guests.

"I appreciate your presence here tonight. After we dine, I've arranged a few exclusive diversions." He paused for effect. "For those interested in a high-stakes game of chance, we have set a private room up for poker. Invitations are limited to senior associates only."

A murmur rippled through the crowd. He continued, "Alternatively, there will be an auction of prized artifacts. Exquisite paintings, rare firearms—all ready for your discerning tastes." The air buzzed with whispered speculations. "And for those of you who'd like to prove your skill, the shooting range is open for a competition. The highest score wins a special prize."

Heads nodded, eyes gleamed. "You're also welcome to retire to your rooms at any point or use our state-of-the-art business center for any urgent matters. Encrypted links are available for your security."

With a last sweep of his gaze, he added, "Tomorrow morning at ten a.m., right here after breakfast, we will officially launch the IronWeb initiative. Enjoy your evening."

Davor Nikolovski stepped back, a dangerous smile on his lips. As his staff guided the guests to their chosen activities, he felt the electric charge of a plan coming together. Then his brow furrowed as he glanced around. He couldn't help but notice the absence of Oleg Sokora—the alias Davor knew Sergei by. Was it a signal of something wrong? Davor gestured for his deputy to come over, pulling him aside.

"What's the word on Sokora?" Davor's voice was low, edged with suspicion.

His deputy shifted. "Message said he's been recalled to Kyiv," he said, fingers sketching air quotes. "I have no clue what's behind it."

Davor's momentary irritation was clear in his expression. Then he exhaled, refocusing on the crucial night ahead. There were bigger games to play, and this was just one piece on a very complicated board. But it was a piece he'd be watching closely.

Davor, Lena, and Igor settled into the control room, a sanctuary of subdued lighting, screens, and encrypted technology. The sturdy leather chairs they occupied formed an unholy trinity at the room's core.

Igor leaned in, cold as Siberian ice. "We've organized a hazardous blend—illegal drugs, firearms, human transport. We have to get everyone on board, make them buy into the future."

Lena, radiating elegance in a sleek, fitted ensemble, idly tapped her fingers on a tablet. "It's all about narrative. As a journalist, I craft stories that move the world. Now, it's time for us to write a tale that will make us untold profits." She delivered the words with the cool confidence of someone who knows how to shape perceptions. "The Black Sun has been pushing to resurrect the glory of the Illyrian empire. If we get Kosovo as our linchpin, our cause gains traction, and the wealth flows even faster."

"Kosovo is the keystone," Davor said in a voice that denied any counter-argument. "Longtime rivals, the Serbians are crucial to success. Get them in and we're not talking about only profit, but mutual power. The Balkans will be under our thumb."

Igor nodded. "Exactly. Secure the Serbians, and the rest of the pieces fall into place."

"We should to stress the security of our routes, the reliability of Serbian corruption," Lena said, fixed on her statistics. "These men we're dealing with may be criminals, but they're also pragmatists. Money talks, but only if you live to spend it."

Davor leaned back, his chair creaking under his

formidable bulk. "Let's not forget Skopje and my homeland, Northern Macedonia. It's more than a source of pride; it's strategic." His eyes seemed like black holes. "Because it's in the heart of the Balkans, this is the ideal spot for us—a gateway for goods from the Middle East and a jump-off point into the European market. And let's be honest, the political climate there is favorable to our business."

Igor's lips curled into a knowing smirk. "Calling the climate favorable hardly does it justice. Your sway in this realm, Davor, is immense."

Lena looked up, a calculated glint in her eye. "Then let's weave that into the narrative. A local hero turns his geopolitical chessboard into an empire. It's poetic. And investors love a story, especially one that comes with a return on investment."

Davor nodded, satisfied. "We've always had an eye for the poetic, haven't we? Skopje becomes our Trojan horse, a signal to all who doubt us. When they see what we've done with my homeland, no one will question our control over Kosovo, Serbia, or any other place we deem ours. Tomorrow, we launch IronWeb," Davor concluded, "and with it, we etch our names into the annals of history. Kosovo is a linchpin, and with it, we'll tie this whole network together."

A palpable electricity filled the room—the kind that comes when a grand ambition is on the brink of becoming reality. Tomorrow would be the day they'd share this vision.

The muted chatter and clinking of glasses in the reception room hushed as the distant thump of helicopter blades sliced through the night air. Davor Nikolovski looked up, frowning. This wasn't on the schedule.

Lena, engrossed in a conversation about media manipulation, paused and turned her head toward the sound. Igor

Kuznetsov, the steely Siberian, also sensed the interruption and stiffened.

Moments later, Davor's second-in-command burst in, urgency etched on his face. "Boss, another chopper is coming in. No heads-up."

"Who is it?" Davor's eyes narrowed.

"Just touched down," the deputy said, earpiece alive with chatter. "It's Alexei Georgiev."

Davor's thoughts whirled. Georgiev, a financial colossus, wielded power that spanned continents. Operating from Sofia, Bulgaria, he was the face of Russia's richest oligarchs in Europe and elsewhere. A puppet master operating from the dark, his involvement introduced an unpredictable element, making the outcome uncertain. Should Georgiev back IronWeb, its prospects for profit could soar.

Georgiev made his entrance, every movement deliberate. Dressed in an exquisite, form-fitting outfit that exuded affluence and authority, he commanded attention. His ice-blue eyes locked with Davor's, charging the room with unspoken queries. This unexpected appearance of Georgiev heightened risks and opportunities. The game had changed.

Davor clasped Georgiev's hand, their firm handshake silently conveying respect. "A surprise, yet not an unwelcome one," Davor mused.

Each understood that what lay ahead in this high-stakes chess game promised not just profit, but also a degree of danger that was impossible to predict.

Later, Davor closed the door, isolating himself in his sanctuary. His room had a combination of natural and elegant features, such as a wooden bed and desk and a bearskin rug he had hunted. He poured himself a glass of single malt and leaned against the desk. His reflection stared back at him from the window, superimposed over the wild terrain and the heavens. It was as if he were peering deep into the core of Iron Hub, and consequently, his IronWeb initiative. The sheer scope of it all weighed on him —the untamed scenery, his sprawling plans, and the complex web of alliances and betrayals.

He took a sip, allowing the warmth to spread from his throat to his unsettled stomach. A restless thought tugged at him. The girl. His hostage. Davor savored the whiskey to calm the chaos in his mind. The temptation became too great.

Stepping out of his personal space, he proceeded down a secure, dimly lit corridor. A retinal scan and a code later, he was looking at the girl through a one-way mirror. Tangled yet lustrous, Paige's blonde hair retained its natural shine. Curled up on a small cot, her lithe figure displayed a mixture of defiance and fear. Though once sun-kissed, her skin now appeared pale under the harsh lighting, yet its softness was unmistakable.

Davor took another swig of whiskey, eyeing the young woman before him. He had expected her to be nothing more than a pawn that he could use, but he already felt drawn towards her spirit and strength. Would she be an asset or a liability? The thought of controlling her fate sent shivers down his spine. He wanted to possess her, yet part of him held back, knowing this decision wasn't so cut and dry.

He stumbled to his bed, achingly aware of the emptiness of the room. The crystal glass he had been sipping his whiskey from sat on the table like a talisman, its contents reflecting the light that streamed through his window. He felt as if the night sky outside were watching him, silently weighing up the choices he would have to face when daybreak finally came. He eventually drifted off to sleep, but it was a fitful one, haunted by a lingering sense of uncertainty.

Chapter 14

Assault on the Accursed Mountains

The Iron Hub loomed in the shadows of the Accursed Mountains, its silhouette a jagged scar against the predawn sky. Creeping fog shrouded the compound, with sparse lights on its facade flickering in the darkness. Cold, metallic, and starkly angular, the Hub exuded an aura of menace.

The air grew colder as Kit and her team inched closer, the scent of frost and pine mingling around them. Occasional clanks and the hushed voices of patrol guards pierced the silence, underscoring the danger that lay ahead. With each step toward the Iron Hub, a knot of anticipation tightened in Kit's stomach, its foreboding presence a silent adversary in their mission. Her breath clouded in the bitter cold.

"You okay?" Dua whispered.

"As good I can be. We're bringing Paige back," Kit replied, her voice tinged with resolve. She thought of Owen, preparing for his part in the operation. "And we've got good backup."

As their boots crunched on the frost-covered gravel,

following the military police, Kit clung to Father Peter's words like a mental talisman. *"The battle belongs to the Lord, and he will deliver all of you into our hands."* Heightened senses, honed from her Tracer Fox, made every sound more acute, from Dua's breathing to the subtle whispers of the wind. She was keenly aware of the predators that roamed these mountains, a threat mirroring the dangers they faced.

The ground, patchy with ice, proved treacherous. Kit's boots skidded, but she swiftly regained her balance. It served as a reminder that their every move was critical.

"We're almost there," Dua murmured, half to herself. "We will bring her back." Hearing Dua's words, and with the first hints of dawn lightening the sky, Kit felt a surge of belief in their mission.

The intelligence that had suggested heightened activity at the Hub increasingly seemed to be accurate. At the lead officer's signal, they dropped to the ground to remain unseen as a patrol passed. As they approached their target, they paused near an iron gate guarded by sentries. Kit Chase's heart raced as she surveyed the barrier. She felt the collective tension of Bravo team, poised for action. Adjusting her gloves, she mentally reviewed their plan: Alpha would create a diversion while Bravo cut the power.

Owen's voice crackled through their earpieces, confirming Alpha team's readiness. Kit exchanged a look with Dua. Taking a deep breath to steady her nerves, adrenaline coursed through her, readying her for the imminent challenge.

With Owen's confirmation resonating in her ears, a signal of readiness, Kit's senses sharpened. The early morning air was thick with a predawn fog, a spectral shroud over the land as she and her team edged closer to the heart of the Iron Hub. The gray mist partly obscured them from any watching eyes as they moved stealthily forward. Her breath formed small, fleeting clouds as she exhaled. The team leader motioned for them to move ahead, each member blending into the darkness. Their steps were softened by the damp ground covered in frost, making it difficult to hear their movements.

Bravo team had flanked the east side of the compound. With a deft touch, they set their charges, and within moments, an almost silent pulse of energy surged through the complex's vulnerable electrical infrastructure. The result was instantaneous. Perimeter lights, once a glow on the horizon, flickered and died, casting the Iron Hub into darkness. The schematics that Kit had retrieved from the drive proved to be accurate, giving them the information they needed. Morozov's last gift—a hard drive filled with schematics—had exposed the hidden nerves and structures of the compound. Armed with this intelligence, Bravo Team's assault was surgical, every step informed by the clear lines of the blueprints.

In the blackout, Kit felt a fresh surge of adrenaline. This was the moment she had prepared for. She knew that inside, the compound would be waking to a pandemonium of confusion and fear. Security systems were now blind, electronic locks released their holds, and the advantage was theirs. It was time to move, to take advantage of the chaos they had crafted.

With night vision goggles over their eyes, they pierced through the darkness, seeing the world in hues of green and black. Kit's mission was clear: infiltrate, extract the hostage, and exfiltrate. Dua and several other officers peeled off, heading for the Iron Hub ops center, while others got into position to deal with the guards. The compound's brief hush belied the fierce resolve Kit felt. This was a rescue, and she would not—could not—let the hostage remain in the clutches of the Iron Hub any longer.

As Kit made her way through the dimly lit corridors, she signaled for the two EUFOR officers trailing behind to hold their positions. "Stay here," she told them in a hushed tone. "I'll confront him first. It might catch him off guard and give us the upper hand. But be ready to act quickly if things go south. I'll signal you when it's time to move." The officers nodded their understanding. They positioned themselves just out of sight, weapons at the ready.

Kit's heart pounded with nervous anticipation as she entered the room alone where Davor stood, his posture smug and threatening, using Paige as a shield. The sight of her cousin's terrified eyes fueled Kit's determination. She squared her shoulders and faced Davor, keeping her tone steady despite the fear bubbling up inside her. "Let her go. We can talk this out."

Davor's laughter echoed off the walls, cold and mocking. "A lone woman? You're either very brave or very foolish." His words sent shivers down Kit's spine, but she refused to show any signs of weakness in front of him. She held her ground, determined to save Paige no matter what it took.

Kit assessed him coolly, her mind racing. She needed to distract him long enough for the officers to intervene without risking Paige. "She's innocent in whatever game you're playing. Release her, and you'll only have to deal with me."

As Davor sneered, dismissing her words, Kit subtly gave the prearranged signal. The EUFOR officers, recognizing the cue, readied themselves. Davor, sensing a shift, glanced around, his grip on Paige tightening. That was when Kit lunged forward in a calculated risk to draw his attention. At that moment, the EUFOR officers burst in. A brief but intense struggle ensued as Davor fought against being arrested. Kit watched with a mix of relief and worry as her team worked to subdue him. She couldn't help but wonder how they would explain this to the higher-ups at EUFOR if Davor was seriously injured.

Finally, they were able to restrain him and lead him out of the room. As he was hauled away, Paige ran into Kit's arms, tears streaming down her face. "Thank you," she whispered.

Kit hugged her tightly before pulling back to inspect any injuries. "Are you okay?"

Paige nodded. "Just scared."

"Me too," Kit admitted with a shaky laugh.

The two women made their way out of the room and towards their extraction point where their team was waiting for them. Kit knew that even in victory there was always danger, and she couldn't let her guard down.

As the ground shook beneath them from a blast, Kit's instincts kicked in. She wrapped a protective arm around Paige, pulling her close and shielding her from the barrage of debris. With her other hand, she fumbled for her flashlight, quickly flicking it on to pierce the darkness.

"You okay?" Kit yelled again over the deafening roar of the explosion's aftermath, her voice filled with urgency. Paige's eyes, wide with shock, met Kit's. She gave a shaky nod, clutching Kit's arm for support.

Kit tried to ensure that Paige was shielded from any potential harm as they navigated the unfamiliar territory, following the EUFOR officers. Every so often, she would cast a quick glance at Paige, checking for any signs of injury.

In the dim glow of her flashlight, Kit navigated through

Iron Hub's labyrinth, guiding Paige to safety. Owen's voice, clear and steady, came through her earpiece. "Head northeast, Kit. We're clearing a path for extraction."

Owen had established a makeshift perimeter, his eyes scanning for Kit and Paige. Their bond, both professional and personal, lent an extra layer of urgency to his watch. As Kit emerged from the maze-like corridors, leading Paige, Owen moved swiftly toward them, a silent understanding passing between them. He quickly checked Paige for injuries before his gaze returned to Kit. Their fingers brushed in a brief, meaningful exchange.

"Where's Dua?" Kit asked.

"Still in the operation room," Owen said, indicating its direction.

"Have there been many arrests?" she asked. She was wondering about Sergei, but she was sure he would have made himself scarce.

"A few. Now we've got Davor, and his mercenaries. But not many notable underworld figures, as far as I know."

"Will you be alright here?" Kit said to Dua. Her cousin looked at Owen and nodded before Kit took off in the direction that Owen had indicated.

At the operation's heart, Dua, flanked by EUFOR officers, was working at the central console. Her fingers flew over the keys, her face etched with fatigue yet marked by resolve. Around her, officers diligently gathered information and equipment. Dua, having successfully completed her vital task, powered down her computer. She allowed herself a moment of satisfaction, eyeing the hard drive that held keys to untold secrets. With a satisfied exhalation, Dua stood, holding up a compact drive, its plain exterior belying its crucial contents.

"Got it," she announced, her voice a mix of exhaustion

and triumph. A collective sigh of relief echoed through the room. The operation now shifted focus. What had begun as a covert operation was now rapidly expanding into a crime scene, with reinforcements securing the area. Davor and his associates were efficiently detained, their expressions a blend of defiance and fear. The Iron Hub buzzed with controlled chaos as teams executed arrest procedures and collected evidence.

As Kit went with Dua, clutching the hard drive under her arm, back to the helipad, she thought about the escape of several key figures in Davor's network. While she couldn't put names to these unseen faces, the conspicuous absence of influential players suggested they had evaded capture, slipping away through well-planned exit strategies. Among those still detained, she caught the eye of Alexei Georgiev, the Bulgarian financier responsible for managing her substantial, albeit confidential, funds. Their gaze was brief but loaded with a mutual recognition of the delicate balance they maintained. To the world, Alexei was just another person caught in the criminal roundup, but to Kit, he was a vital link to her hidden financial world. She moved past him, carefully avoiding any interaction that could unravel their carefully constructed façade.

With the mission's critical goals achieved, the exhausted Alpha and Bravo teams made their way to the designated extraction point. Above them, EUFOR helicopters hovered, their rotors slicing through the frigid air in the cold light of dawn.

As she waited for the loading of their helicopter, Kit stood to one side, her fingers instinctively finding the pendant around her neck. Hanging from a slim gold chain was a small, worn cross, a keepsake from Father Peter. Its ancient surface, worn by time and prayer, seemed to echo with silent stories and secrets. It reminded her of the meditation that he had also given her, that had brought her this far. She caught Dua's attention. "We need to analyze that drive promptly. It could reveal much more."

"Count on it," Dua said with a grin.

Together, the women moved toward the helicopter. Paige, now safe and attended by medics, offered Kit a smile tinged with gratitude and relief as they boarded.

"Next time, promise you won't let me out of your sight?" Paige half-joked, though her eyes betrayed the fear she had faced.

Kit squeezed her cousin's hand reassuringly. "You have my word."

Paige's concern shifted. "Mom's going to be frantic."

"I haven't broken the news yet," Kit admitted, meeting Paige's eyes with a mix of regret and relief.

Paige's voice trembled slightly. "That's probably for the best. Otherwise she would have been beside herself with worry. I just want to be back for Christmas."

"I knew we'd find you. And we'll make Christmas special here in Kosovo," Kit assured her.

Dua, leaning in against the drone of the engines, added, "We found solid evidence linking Davor Nikolovski to the Christmas market tragedy."

Kit's focus sharpened. "What kind of evidence?"

"Photographic confirmation of the kill from the assassin and incriminating emails," Dua said.

"The CIA and NATO will need to see this," Kit said thoughtfully. "Make sure it's thoroughly documented and secure duplicates."

"So, was it rescuing me or snagging the bad guys that excited you more?" Paige asked, lightening the mood.

Kit looked at Paige, her eyes serious. "Getting you back was the priority. Everything else is a bonus."

Paige exhaled with a mix of drama and relief. "Guess I shouldn't complain about life back in New Zealand, huh?"

"Nope," Kit replied with a grin, and a ripple of laughter lightened the cabin, offering a brief respite from the intensity of their ordeal.

Chapter 15

The Debrief

Inside the EUFOR Operational Center in Pristina, the usual buzz of activity had been replaced by a focused and tense silence. The monitors displayed drone footage from the Iron Hub, now transformed into a bustling center for forensic investigation. In one corner, a slightly wrinkled EUFOR flag served as a reminder of their crucial mission. The room was commanded by Major Matt Hackman, his posture a mixture of exhaustion and determination. His uniform showed evidence of a sleepless night. Nearby, Kit's usually immaculate appearance was now rumpled and marked with signs of the operation. On the other side of the room, Eva was deeply immersed in preliminary reports, her expression a combination of concentration and relief. Don Edgson and Max, embodying a hard-earned sense of victory, readied themselves for the debrief with confidence and readiness.

Taking a deep breath, Hackman commenced the debriefing. "Mission outcomes: Paige White extracted successfully. We've unearthed evidence connecting the Black Sun group and the Siberian Vipers. Davor

Nikolovski and associates are in custody, but some suspects have evaded capture. As for Bulgarian financier, Alexei Georgiev, he's been released, thanks to his legal team."

Kit twirled her pen, a thoughtful expression on her face. "Georgiev's role?"

"From what we can tell, there is no direct evidence against him. He's free now," Owen said.

"Maybe our focus should shift towards the bigger fish, like the Christmas market case," she suggested.

Eva, spreading photos on the table, added, "Tracing the funds is key. We suspect Georgiev's financial ties to Nikolovski but need hard evidence. It's a matter of piecing it all together."

Kit nodded. "Any leads on the Black Sun's connections with the Siberian Vipers? And Jacob Mueller?"

Dua, with Hackman's nod, displayed data fragments. Owen, typically the presenter, aided her. "Evidence suggests a potential alliance. A 'J. Mueller' is referenced, but we can't confirm it's our Jacob Mueller yet."

Kit thought back to the thumb drive she'd recently turned in.

"We're dissecting that data. If it ties Mueller to money laundering, it could impact his case in Germany." She then returned to the evidence linking Davor, the Black Sun, and Siberian Vipers to recent crimes. "The evidence is compelling, but we must ensure its good enough to stand up in court," she concluded.

The rhythm of the debrief was interrupted by a new arrival—Katya Petrova. Her poised elegance in contrast to the weary field agents, she gracefully took her seat. "I have been assigned to oversee the report for the OIDC deputy head of mission," she announced.

Kit's eyes briefly met Eva's. Their shared glance echoed Kit's lingering doubts about Katya's true loyalties.

"Your concerns will be addressed, Ms. Petrova. Full transparency with the deputy head of mission is our priority," Eva said.

"That is reassuring to hear," she replied.

As the meeting continued to examine the evidence, Kit's attention subtly shifted at the sound of a discreet alert from her device. With practiced composure, she glanced at the incoming message from Sergei, her grip on the device tightening just slightly. The message was succinct: "Surveillance confirms Katya met with an unknown Black Sun affiliate last night. Caution advised. S."

Kit's fingers paused over the keyboard as the significance of Sergei's message settled in her mind. In the quiet hum of the conference room filled with murmurs and the shuffle of papers, she felt a chill that had nothing to do with the winter air outside. This new piece of intelligence was a stark reminder that the game of espionage they were all entangled in was far from over. The meeting was drawing to a close, and with it, the illusion of order and resolution they had all been grasping at. As the last of the evidence was presented and the officials began to disperse with a sense of accomplishment, Kit remained anchored in her seat, her thoughts adrift in the murky waters of uncertainty.

Kit had played a pivotal role in unraveling the complex web of crime, leading to the disruption of the sinister alliance between the Iron Hub, the Siberian Vipers, and the Black Sun. Her efforts had not only solved the grisly murder that set everything in motion but had also landed some key players behind bars, crippling their ambitious criminal enterprise. However, a tangle of unresolved mysteries lingered in the cold winter air. The potential involvement of

Kit's former boss, Jacob Mueller, with the Black Sun loomed ominously, raising questions about the depth of corruption within the ranks of those trusted to protect. Furthermore, the unpredictable moves of the Black Sun remained a shadowy threat on the horizon.

In the midst of these uncertainties, personal dilemmas intertwined with professional ones. Kit pondered the enigmatic motives of Katya from the FSB, whose actions within the OIDC were as cryptic as they were critical. The evolution of her relationships with Owen and the enigmatic Russian agent, Sergei, added layers complexity to her already tangled personal life. As she delved deeper into the nuances of khash philosophy, seeking enlightenment in its teachings, she wondered how these insights would shape her future decisions. And in the background, the potential path of her cousin Paige loomed. Would she too be drawn into the labyrinth of law and justice, following in Kit's footsteps? Each question was a thread in Kit's life, weaving a pattern that was yet to be fully revealed.

Chapter 16

Deck the Halls with Laughter

The apartment was bathed in the warm glow of Christmas cheer, filled with the comforting scent of pine. In one corner, a richly green spruce stood majestically, its branches adorned with an eclectic mix of traditional baubles and handicrafts from the women's collective. Dua and Paige had lavished care on its decoration, intertwining silver tinsel and strings of delicate white lights that cast an enchanting shimmer across the room. A golden star perched at the top, flickering softly in the festive light.

Amid the laughter and chatter, the ringtone of Kit's laptop pierced the air. She quickly attended to the incoming video call, revealing the sunlit faces of her mother, Rosalyn, and her sister, Jen, who was also Paige's mother, from New Zealand.

"Happy Christmas from down under!" Rosalyn's voice rang out, full of festive spirit. "Sending love from the future. It's Christmas afternoon here! How's life in Kosovo, Paige? We've missed hearing from you since you arrived in Pristina."

Paige hesitated, a shadow momentarily dimming her smile before she regained her composure. "It's been quite the journey," she said. "And you won't believe it. We have a real white Christmas here! It's so different from our sunny Decembers back home."

The conversation flowed naturally, peppered with laughter and lighthearted family banter. As Rosalyn and Jen recounted tales of their holiday preparations, Paige's expression mingled nostalgia with a deep sense of gratitude.

Glancing out the window, Paige's eyes sparkled at the sight of snowflakes gently descending over Pristina. "It's snowing!" she exclaimed. "I wish you could see this."

After exchanging final words and promises to reconnect soon, the screen went dark. Paige lingered on the closed laptop, her longing for home briefly surfacing in her gaze.

The group then gathered for their Secret Santa gift exchange around a table laden with festively wrapped presents. The air was filled with a blend of holiday spirit and a deeper, unspoken connection born from their shared experiences. Amidst the cozy warmth of the apartment, they took turns distributing gifts. Dua received a beautiful scarf, Owen unwrapped handcrafted wooden coasters, and Natalia was delighted with a hand-painted ceramic mug.

Kit's turn brought a medium-sized, elegantly wrapped box in deep forest green with a golden ribbon. The room hushed in anticipation as she carefully unwrapped it, revealing a handcrafted, leather-bound journal. Its pages were thick and inviting, ideal for capturing thoughts and memories. A note tucked inside read: "For the stories yet to be told."

Kit's eyes shone with appreciation. "I love it! Journalling is one of my favorite things," she said, hugging it to her chest, touched by the thoughtfulness of the gift.

Paige then brought out homemade mince pies, their flaky crusts and rich fruit filling infused with a hint of brandy, filling the air with a tantalizing aroma. She also unveiled a Christmas cake adorned with glazed cherries and almond marzipan. "I smuggled the marzipan from home," she chuckled. "Good thing customs didn't check my bag!"

Kit had been waiting for a moment during the group's Secret Santa exchange. Her personal gift for Owen was carefully wrapped and caught his curious gaze as she presented it to him. As he carefully unwrapped the gift, a slim, antique pocket watch was revealed. The silver casing boasted intricate engravings, showcasing its rich history and skilled craftsmanship. When Owen opened the watch, he found an engraved message inside that read, "Every second counts." He looked up at Kit, and in that moment, they shared a wordless understanding of unspoken bonds and a cherished past that was as timeless as the gift in Owen's hands.

In the background, soft instrumental music filled the room, a rendition of "Deck the Halls" playing. The melody, reminiscent of the calming frequencies used in Father Peter's khash meditations, enveloped the room in a soothing yet uplifting aura.

As the group indulged in Paige's homemade delicacies, they basked in the moment's peace. This simple gathering was a testament to the bond forged through their shared experiences and challenges. While they planned to head to the Hopscotch Bar later, for now, Kit's apartment was the perfect sanctuary, a place to create and savor cherished memories in the midst of their demanding lives.

. . .

The Hopscotch Bar provided the ideal setting for the team's post-mission celebration, combining a cozy charm with an upscale ambiance. The warm glow of vintage light fixtures set against exposed brick walls created a welcoming atmosphere, complemented by festive decorations and the comforting scents of cinnamon and pine.

As they walked in, Gavin, the Scottish bartender, welcomed them warmly. His white shirt and black vest perfectly matched the bar's atmosphere. "Ah, look who's graced us with their presence, the VIPs! You've arrived just in time for the celebrations!" he announced, his friendly nod instantly creating a laid-back atmosphere for the evening.

Don had reserved a spacious table. Kit's group from the apartment arrived, and the bar filled with delight. Major Matt Hackman, in his off-duty attire, organized the seating to ensure everyone was comfortable. Eva Refavo, Axel Delcroix, Christina Wackelnagel, and Angel exchanged lighthearted conversations and shared in the joyful moment.

Major Hackman raised his glass first, toasting, "To those who dare, and those who overcome!" Eva followed, honoring her heritage with, "*Alla giustizia e alla verità*, to justice and truth!" Kit, true to her ethos, added, "Keep chasing justice!"

Gavin chimed in with his signature charm. "Here's to nights filled with laughter and a wee bit of the unexpected!" He began serving rounds of "The Hero's Elixir," a potent concoction of Scottish whisky and elderflower liqueur, sweetened with honey-ginger syrup—a tribute to courage.

As the evening progressed, the bar was alive with stories of past missions, a mix of intense experiences and light-hearted anecdotes. Angel, catching the vibe, queued up a selection of classic hits and holiday tunes on the jukebox, prompting some to dance.

Katya Petrova leaned casually against the bar, her observant gaze sweeping over the group. Her connections with senior management and rumored links to the Russian FSB spy service created a subtle yet noticeable distance from the rest. However, Brad Harris, the deputy head of mission, approached her with two glasses of Hero's Elixir in hand.

The night's atmosphere mellowed as Katya and Brad gradually integrated with the group, sharing in the laughter and storytelling, setting aside suspicions for a moment of shared humanity.

Later in the evening, Kit slipped outside for some fresh air. Standing with her glass in hand on the Hopscotch Bar terrace, she gazed out at the cityscape. The neon lights painted streaks of vitality across the night, and the sporadic honking of car horns punctuated the city's ever-present heartbeat. Yet, amidst this urban orchestra, a rare stillness embraced her. Paige emerged, the door closing softly behind her, and stepped beside Kit, her breath fogging in the crisp air. She raised her glass, its clink against Kit's cutting through the quiet.

Paige nodded. "I never imagined ... When I wanted to follow in your footsteps, I didn't know it would mean literally surviving a murder investigation and kidnapping."

Kit chuckled, her breath visible in the cold air. "Neither did I, but then, justice doesn't follow a script. It's messy, unpredictable."

A comfortable silence fell between them,.

Paige glanced back towards the bar. "I used to think the

law was black-and-white. But this ... it's like living in a twilight world."

Kit nodded, her gaze following Paige's. "It's those spaces between day and night that can teach us the most. They challenge us to find the clarity in our convictions."

They stood a while longer, each lost in thought. Then, as if on cue, they turned back toward the warm glow of the pub.

"Shall we?" Kit gestured with a tilt of her head towards the door.

Paige smiled. "After àll, we can't let the others celebrate without us."

As they stepped inside, the sound of laughter and music welcomed them back. Some of Kit's colleagues raised glasses in a silent salute to their return. The contrast of the lively atmosphere inside with the city view on the terrace encapsulated the essence of their Christmas. In a world fraught with risks, loyalty, and secrecy, they found solace in the company of their group and the strength of their family ties, no matter the distance between them.

-THE END-

More Books by Tasmin Turner

Thank you for journeying alongside Kit on this thrilling adventure. If you enjoyed the experience, I'd greatly appreciate it if you could spare a moment to rate and review the book on your preferred platform. Your feedback truly makes a difference!

Here's a glance at what lies ahead in the Crime Scene Kosovo series:

1. *The Missing Diary*
2. *The Price of Justice*
3. *Explosive Reprisals*

A potential fourth installment, tentatively titled *In Plain View*, is currently being contemplated.

In addition, I'm excited to reveal that seasonal novellas kicked off with a special Halloween edition, *Halloween and the Black Sun*. The next to look forward to? *A Kosovo Valentine's Day* is being crafted to bring another riveting twist to Kit's saga.

Stay connected and immerse yourself further into the world of Crime Scene Kosovo! For the latest updates on new releases, giveaways, and exclusive pre-release specials, sign up for the newsletter at www.wish-books.com or email joann@dreamlifenz.com. Engage with me and fellow fans on Facebook at www.facebook.com/CrimeSceneKS/, where you can share your thoughts, participate in discussions, enjoy updates, and gain insights into the series. Your support fuels the journey, and I can't wait to continue sharing Kit's adventures with you.

Stay tuned, and thank you once more for being a part of this thrilling ride!

Until next time, keep chasing justice!

Tasmin Turner

About Tasmin Turner

Tasmin Turner is the author of the Crime Scene Kosovo Series, which is based in the early 2000s in post-conflict Balkans. Tasmin lives in the heartland of New Zealand, after two decades of living in Europe and the US. She's passionate about writing and enjoys frequenting cafés.

Author's Note
Information about Kosovo

The Crime Scene Kosovo series is set in a fictional post-conflict Kosovo, with fictitious characters, organizations, and events. The information below is a brief account of Kosovo's real historical background.

Kosovo is a self-declared independent country in Europe's Balkan region. Although many nations—including the United States and several members of the European Union—acknowledge its 2008 declaration of freedom from Serbia, Russia and some other countries, including some EU states, do not recognize Kosovo's independence. Most inhabitants are Albanian, and the minority are Serbs, together with other ethnic minority groups. The official languages are Albanian and Serbian.

The name Kosovo is derived from a Serbian term meaning "field of blackbirds." After serving as the heart of a medieval kingdom of Serbia, Kosovo was governed by the Ottoman Empire from the mid-fifteenth century to the early twentieth century. This was an era when Islam grew in importance and the number of Albanian speakers in the region grew. Then, in the early twentieth century, Kosovo was incorporated into Serbia (later part of Yugoslavia). By the second half of that century, Muslims of Albanian origin outnumbered Eastern Orthodox Serbs in Kosovo, leading to frequent interethnic tensions in the province.

In 1998, an ethnic, Albanian-led secessionist rebellion escalated into a global crisis, resulting in NATO's 1999 air bombardment of Yugoslavia, which at that time was a remnant state composed of Serbia and Montenegro. Peace was restored afterward, and Kosovo was administered by the United Nations and supported by several other international and regional organizations during post-conflict times.

A landlocked country, Kosovo is flanked by Serbia to the north and east, North Macedonia to the south, Albania to the west, and Montenegro to the northwest. About the same geographic size as Jamaica or Lebanon, Kosovo is one of the smallest countries in the Balkans, with a population of less than two million people in 2021, predominantly of Albanian descent. The capital, Pristina, is also the largest urban area. Albanian and Serbian are spoken languages, with most Kosovars adhering to Sunni Islam.

The information in this description is drawn from the following source: John B. Allcock, Antonia Young, and John R. Lampe. "Kosovo." *Encyclopedia Britannica* (8 Nov. 2022). https://www.britannica.com/place/Kosovo.

9 781738 616428